A Soul to Take

Amber Fisher

Blue Demon Media

Copyright © 2019 by Amber Fisher

All rights reserved.

No part of this book may be reproduced in any form or by any electronic or mechanical means, including information storage and retrieval systems, without written permission from the author, except for the use of brief quotations in a book review.

For Zachary, without whom this book would have been a lot cringier.

CHAPTER ONE

May 13th

T HE AUDIENCE IS REVERENT as they shuffle through the close-cut grass, their voices just above whispers as they check their programs and filter down the aisles. They're dressed conservatively in dark colors, shoulders and knees covered, men in suits and ties. Even the children look somber as their parents harangue them into appropriate behavior, scolding them if they laugh too loudly. Occasions like this are not meant for screaming, wild children, though the kids don't understand. They want to run and jump. Mothers press their charges into their seats, promising that when the ceremony is over, there will be plenty of time to play. But for now, they must sit and pay their respects. That's what they're here to do.

The aisles are arranged by color: overlarge bouquets of pink flowers on the right, the same bouquets on the left but in orange. As the attendees flow into the area, they stammer and frown, pointing and gesturing before choosing a seat. No one wants to be too close to the front; that's reserved for the closest members of the family, and it would be disrespectful to horn in on that intimate space. But sitting too far in the back looks bad, too, like they're ready to make a quick escape. Somewhere in the middle is best. They want to put their best face forward, a unified show of support, even though almost all of them would rather be anywhere else than here.

Music floats softly from the speakers; it's nothing I recognize. Something bland and traditional that's probably supposed to feel sophisticated. It makes me anxious, and I can tell it's having a similar effect on the other invitees. Although, I really shouldn't say "other" invitees, since that makes it sound like I've been invited.

I haven't. But crashing events like these is sometimes necessary.

The cheap folding chairs are beginning to fill up as families and friends make their way to their seats, husbands and wives bickering in hushed tones as they decide who will sit where. Single men and women sit wherever they want, casually glancing at their phones for the time. The event should be starting, but as surprises no one, the officiant is nowhere to be seen. Minutes pass almost audibly, and I survey the audience, most of them looking as bored and fretful as I feel.

After a long while, the music changes. It's about time. I roll my eyes as a solemn hush falls over the crowd. Even the children are still, their little faces drawn and dark as finally, all heads turn to the back where a procession has begun. The audience turns on their appropriate faces, some tearful, others passive, some serene. They watch the procession until the music changes once again, and everyone stands up.

At the back of the garden, a woman in a huge white gown appears with a tuxedoed man at her side. As they begin their dramatic, carefully-paced walk down the aisle, my heart seizes in my chest.

Jesus Christ, this is a wedding.

I curse quietly, not wanting to draw attention to myself. It isn't the first time that I've been sent to what's supposed to be a joyful occasion, and I'm sure it won't be the last. But dammit, a little heads up would be nice. Though I suppose if they gave me that kind of information, I might choose not to show up.

And then they'd really be up a creek, wouldn't they?

Perhaps not. Probably they'd just send someone else. It's not like I'm a particularly rare breed or anything.

The audience has returned to their seats and the bride and groom are holding hands, staring goopily into each other's eyes as the officiant drones on about love and destiny and the welfare of the human race. I don't know if that's really what he's saying. I'm not exactly listening. My eyes are peeled for my target. After all, I wasn't sent here to participate in the joys of matrimonial bondage.

I'm here to kill someone.

Nearly twenty minutes into the ceremony, I begin to wonder whether I've gotten some bad information. I don't see any indication that any of the people here are supposed to die today. Everyone looks healthy, if somewhat distracted, and I don't see a single silver cord with my name on it. I'm getting antsy and ready to go back home when a man in the very back of the garden and dressed in street clothes starts moving forward. He makes it as far as the second-to-last row of chairs before calling out, "Don't say till death do you part, Sharon."

A murmur ripples through the crowd as the officiant abruptly stops speaking, and all bodies turn around to get an eyeful of the man with the audacity to interrupt the wedding. It only takes a moment for the gasps to begin, the sharp intakes of breath as some of the audience recognize the man.

Well, now that I get a better look, I'm not sure if they're gasping because they recognize him or because he's pointing a rifle at the bride and groom.

"You said that to me, once," he says, taking a small step forward, rifle butt against his shoulder as he stares down the sights. "You said till death do us part, but here you are, still alive, about to marry somebody else. So don't listen to her," he says, apparently addressing the groom, who has stepped forward to place his body in front of his bride. His face has gone to ash. "Nothing that bitch says can be trusted."

All of a sudden, the air splits apart. The loudest sound I've ever heard cracks through the evening as the screams begin and the groom topples to the floor. A second crack follows quickly on, and the bride drops next, a garish circle of red blooming over her bosom, the white fabric going to pink at its edges like tie-dye. The audience is screaming now, leaping from chairs and tearing away from the madman with the gun. But I don't watch them. None of the screaming people interests me. The screamers are all alive and destined to live. It's the quiet ones at the front of the garden that I'm interested in.

Everything has begun to grow soft and hazy, and as the air around the altar and overturned folding chairs turns thin and iridescent, I make my transition. It's time. I glide toward the fallen couple, my movements quick and practiced as I search for their silver cords. The groom's cord spills from the back of his left shoulder, and I follow its line straight up into heaven, an unbroken thing carrying no tag with my name on it. The groom lives, then. Lucky him.

I turn my attention to the woman lying next to him, blood seeping into the grass beneath her. As I inch closer to her, I hear her whimpering, her attempt at making words forming bubbles of blood at her lips. Her eyes are still open, and if I didn't know better, I'd say she's looking right at me, but I know that can't be right. I've transitioned into my death skin, and I'm invisible once I've donned it. I turn my ear closer to her, hoping to catch her dying words. "I love you," she says. Her eyelids flutter but do not close. The irises are large and brown, so glassy I can see myself in them like mirrors.

I tear my gaze away from her face to seek out her silver cord. Hers is attached at the base of her neck beneath the carefully coiffed hairline. Her veil somewhat obscures it, so I gingerly nudge the fabric aside. I have to be sure she's my target.

Beneath the gauzy material is my name tag attached to her silver cord, marking her as the person whose soul I am to take today. I heave a sigh. "I'm sorry," I say, though the words come out as mild chirps, nothing any human could hope to understand. "It isn't personal. It's just business."

I hop onto her back, clip her silver cord into my beak, and tug until her soul comes loose, drifting from her body. As soon as I have it, I feel her heartbeat beneath my talons come to a slow stop, the susurrations of her thready breathing ceasing altogether. Her last breath leaves her lungs as I launch myself into the sky, my beak piercing through the shimmering veil that has descended, the veil that makes everything hazy and dim, the veil that only appears at the time of death, a portal between the worlds of the living and the dead. I spread my wings and soar heavenward with the bride's howling soul in my beak and the cries of the wedding-goers at my back. It isn't how I would have wanted this death to play out, but then, orchestrating the circumstances of death is not my job. My job is to bring it.

I am a raven.

And I kill people.

CHAPTER TWO

October 5th

I HAVE LIVED IN AUSTIN, TEXAS, all my life. I know this city like the underside of my wing. I know the best places for food, the best places to listen to live music, and the best venues for people-watching. The latter activity is by far my favorite. I know that may seem morbid since, as a reaper, my job is to take human lives. But I suppose you could call it an occupational hazard that since my work is so closely tied to your lives—or, more aptly, to your demise—I've come to feel tender towards you.

Killing you brings me no joy; lately, it's precisely the opposite. I loathe every reap I'm sent on, and each life I take brings me one step closer to lying in the middle of Mo-Pac during rush hour until I'm run over by a rideshare driver.

Actually, rush hour is a terrible time to try to get run over. Cars crawl by; the momentum would probably just maul me, and with my luck, I'd live. I should aim to kill myself on a Saturday morning when cars can scream down the highway at 80mph. That's a much better plan, now that I think of it.

Today, I'm flying over Pease Park where the city is hosting

an Oktoberfest event. Oktoberfest is a goldmine for birds like me: it means drunk people dropping food everywhere, and not just any food. Oktoberfest means bratwursts and—my personal favorite—pretzels. Salty, soft, and full of butter, you really can't go wrong with a delicious pretzel. I glide lower, following my nose until I find what I'm looking for: a gathering of three adults with a couple of children in tow. One of the women carries a handful of pretzels. If I can get close enough without looking too intimidating, perhaps they'll be kind and throw a few nibbles my way. But as I near, I realize they're having an argument. That means I might have to wait for a treat. But I can be patient.

"That's easy for you to say, Candace, because you're not the one that would have to take care of her." The man speaking has dark hair and darker eyes. His arms are folded across his chest, his eyes narrowed to a slit. "So you'll have to forgive me if your opinion on the matter isn't, you know, sacrosanct."

I lick the edges of my beak as a thrill runs through me. You don't live among humans for as long as I have without learning to recognize family drama when you see it. I've had plenty of practice sussing out family disagreements, lover's spats, and coworker squabbles. See, I am an unrepentant eavesdropper. Listening in on other people's conversations is one of the only things I look forward to these days. Human drama and human food. Everything else is pure misery.

"It's *not* easy for me to say, because even though I won't be the one taking care of her, I *will* be the one footing the bill. I don't see either one of you stepping up to the plate to take on this—by the way—*tremendous* expense."

The man gives a short bark of laughter and rolls his eyes. "You *volunteered* the money! Nobody asked you to do that."

Candace makes a sound of disgust in the back of her throat. "If I don't do it, who will? You're the biggest tightwad I've ever seen, Andrew. And even if you weren't, I doubt your shrew wife would let you pay for Mom's care."

The other woman, the one who's been silent so far, heaves a deep sigh and glances at the other two. "I don't think now is an appropriate time to talk about this," she says, gesturing with her eyebrows toward the children in their proximity. "Can't we do this later? I thought we came out here to have a good time. Why don't you guys go get a couple of beers? Bring me back something good. And by that, I mean not an IPA." She rolls her eyes as she says this, a hint of laughter forming around her words.

But Andrew makes no move to leave. Instead, he squints at this second woman speaking and says, "No offense, but this doesn't concern you, Carrie. Nobody expects you to take care of Mom. You don't have the money or the…capacity."

Carrie's eyes go momentarily wide in surprise before her whole face settles into a grimace. "If y'all want to argue about what to do with Mom without me, that's fine. I *thought* you wanted my input because I *am* part of this family. I thought that—"

"Jesus Christ, Carrie, way to make this all about you when it's *not about you*." It's the first woman—Candace—speaking. "It's not that we don't value your opinion." Oh, it clearly is. "It's just that you don't have as much skin in the game. Nobody's asking you to make huge financial investments. Nobody's asking you to give up what free time you have to take care of her. Do you know how exhausting it is to take care of children *and* Mom at the same time? It's unfair," Candace says, her face flushing, "but no, you wouldn't know that. You can't understand, because all you *have* is free time."

The look on Carrie's face is so filled with anguish that my heart leaps out for her. Her eyes are flat with hurt, and her cheeks glow hot with embarrassment. She opens her mouth to speak but closes it again, nostrils flaring. Finally, she shakes her head, her whole body trembling as she says, "Go to hell, Candace. Just really go straight to hell."

Carrie turns to leave, and Andrew throws Candace a look I

can't read. The bitchy sister rolls her eyes and motions for Andrew to follow Carrie. I follow behind, and not just because Carrie's the one with the pretzels. I want to know how this plays out. He follows his sister into the trees, her face upturned to the sky, blinking back tears of frustration. He reaches out to touch her shoulder, but Carrie bats his hand away, scowling.

"Thanks for nothing!" she snaps. "You could have said something. But I don't know why I expected anything different. This is how all of you think of me. *'Oh, Carrie is such a fuck-up. Carrie can't do anything right. We can't let Carrie have an opinion on Mom's care because if we leave it up to her, she'll probably start hearing voices and then drown herself in the lake.'*"

Andrew doesn't bristle at the admonishment. If anything, he looks mildly bored. He steps forward and pulls his sister into a hug; this time, she lets him. The pretzels squish between their chests. "Candace could have been nicer about what she said," he agrees as she snivels against his shoulder. "But I understand where she's coming from. After all—"

"I can help, though. If you guys would stop trying to ease me out, I could help. I mean, yeah, I don't have money, but I have…time…"

Andrew makes a face, sighing as he releases his sister. "Carrie, maybe it's better if you just let Candace handle everything, you know? I mean, you've got enough stress in your life. You don't want to end up back at…*you* know. I mean, you're still dealing with the…miscarriage and all."

Carrie's face blanches as her mouth drops open. She takes a step backward, holding up a finger in protest. Her voice is flat and low and even when she speaks. "That has *nothing* to do with any of this, and screw you for even bringing it up. I told you about all that in confidence. You didn't say anything to Candace, did you?"

Andrew opens his mouth, then clamps it shut. The veins in his neck stand out, and it's obvious even to me that he has. Carrie's expression is incredulous. "You *told* her? How *could* you? I don't want Candace to know about every goddamn miscarriage—"

"I don't know why you won't let her help," he interrupts, barely disguising his exasperation. "She's a *doctor*. She knows something here. She says that having this many miscarriages isn't normal. She says—"

"I don't give a good goddamn what good doctor Candace has to say about my miscarriages, you son of a bitch. If I wanted her advice, I'd go to her. She couldn't do *anything* for me after the stillbirth. Her way of helping was to convince my husband to put me away for a while. So if you think I want her help *now*, you're nuts."

Andrew swallows and licks his lips. He rubs the back of his neck as he looks around, helpless. "The stillbirth thing was two years ago, Carrie," he says. "I'm not saying you should get over it. I'm just saying—"

"You goddamn better not be saying I should get over it!" she shouts, her voice breaking with emotion. "You don't have any idea the hell I've been through! I carried that baby for nine months with absolutely no hint of a problem. You have three healthy kids, and you've never had to do anything but screw your wife to get them. So don't stand there and lecture *me* about how I should be feeling or whether or not I should be dealing with it better! You have no idea what you're talking about!"

Andrew shakes his head, his shoulders sagging. He's grown weary under the weight of this conversation; he looks like a dog that's been kicked. He should drop it, but the look in his eyes tells me he won't. Sometimes I wish for human vocal cords so that I could inform clueless men when it's time to pack it in. "Carrie. Just listen to me a minute, will you? You had a lot going on. You guys were moving, and Jake's new job was stressful...I mean, you weren't really doing everything you could...? Look, I'm not blaming you." He is. "I'm not saying he died because of you." You totally are. "It's just—"

Carrie throws the pretzels on the ground, covers her ears with her hands, and screams. For a moment, I'm torn between the pretzels and the drama, but in the end, the drama wins. "All any of you have done for the past two years is blame me! *'Carrie, you can't eat vegan while you're pregnant. You should have known better. Carrie, you can't do yoga while you're pregnant, it's too stressful for the baby. Carrie, you can't travel while you're pregnant, it cuts off circulation to the baby.'* I've heard so many goddamn excuses from you and Candace about all the things I did wrong. I don't need another lecture. It's taken me this long to conclude that all of you are full of shit, and *I didn't do anything wrong.* Sometimes terrible things happen, and there isn't anyone to blame for it." That's right. "It's just fate." It is. "It's just fucking fate."

I couldn't have said it better myself.

The sadness in her words is what finally does it, and Andrew relents, remorseful. "Maybe you're right," he says. "Maybe it wasn't anything you did. I'm just…I'm trying to help. So I'm just saying, you know. Maybe you should just let it go."

"Maybe I should let it go," Carrie agrees, running her hands through her hair. "Maybe that's what I should do. After all, you're right about something: I am a complete fuck-up. I couldn't make it through college. I spent eight months in the loony bin. I lost my baby. Multiple times. Multiple babies. So yeah, you're right: I am a complete fuck-up. But one thing I know for sure. The baby that *died in my arms* wasn't my goddamn fault."

Carrie turns then, and her cold eyes fall on me. In a split second, her expression changes from sorrowful to stunned. Her eyes laser-focus on me, and for a moment, I'm sure that someone or something must be behind me, that she can't be directing her attention to *me* of all things. But she is. Her voice rattles when she says, "White feathers."

Andrew blinks and stammers, his face full of questions. "Feathers? Huh?"

Carrie ignores him as she continues to stare daggers at me. I take a fretful step backward as tension grows thick in the air around us. "That raven has white feathers at his beak."

Now I *know* she's talking about me. It's an anomaly from birth, these white feathers along the right side of my beak. I've always been slightly embarrassed by them, but I've never thought a human would notice them. After all, when it comes to black birds, you humans are woefully unable to tell us apart. Whether raven, jackdaw, crow, or grackle, you interchange our species with wild abandon. All look same.

But this woman is glaring at me as though she knows me. "The baby was *your* goddamn fault," she says. She points a finger and takes a step nearer to me. In my confusion, I don't even think to step away. "You were there that day, weren't you? You came in through the window, and before my baby could even take his first breath, you snatched him away from me. I tried for *years* to have that baby. And you came in and took everything away."

Andrew sounds as gentle and calm as a hostage negotiator as he says, "Carrie, what are you talking about? Are you okay? Do you need to sit down for a second? I can get you some water—"

"I'm not talking to you," she says, her eyes still focused on me. "I'm talking to him."

Now, Andrew looks to me, his brow furrowed. "You're talking to the *bird?*"

"Yes," she says. "He was there that day. Ravens are bad omens. They bring death. And he was there that day. Weren't you?"

In all the years I have been tending to the lives and deaths in Austin, no one has ever confronted me about my business. No one has ever accused me of killing their child, even on the occasions where it was true. And I am so startled by her accusation that I am about to fly away in protest when it comes to me.

I do know this woman.

Two Years Ago

IT WAS AN UNSEASONABLY COOL, clear morning in the foothills of Austin. I was out for my morning soar, stretching my wings and letting the wind carry me. I smelled wet, rotting leaves, fecund earth—the smell of autumn.

I dropped lower as the wind died down until I could see the pretty houses dotting the hillside—Xeriscaped lawns, SUVs or minivans in the driveways, organic vegetable gardens in the backyard. I knew the sort—they flourished in Travis county. The Earth-aware, alternative medicine, sustainable types. Many of the houses had children's toys in the front yards, indicating early-rising rapscallions within. But one home, the one where my business lay that morning, stirred in its own way even as the other houses slept.

A woman's voice, guttural and animal-like, cried out.

Sweeping down toward the house, I smelled sweat, blood, and anxiety. Even from outside its walls, the house seemed to exude a feral stench. The energy was frenzied, frenetic. I could hear two voices: one soft and comforting and another that cried out in pain.

I circumnavigated the house several times trying to get my bearings before I saw the open window. I offered silent words of thanks to She Who Makes My Work Possible.

I know her as the Virago, the tempest whose whims dictate the world's destiny. But she has many other names besides. Some call her Fate, or Chance, or the Wheel of Fortune. I've also heard her called Bitch, Cunt, Whore. None of these is right, and all of them are.

She's a skilled weaver of chance and circumstance, that one. I can't very well get into homes to perform my death ritual if the windows are closed. I need the Virago to leave her whispers of suggestion, her nudges toward unusual behavior. *It's too warm*, she might have whispered. *Such lovely weather.* And then someone suddenly found themselves uncomfortably flushed inside this sleepy house, opening a window just enough for an avian of death to enter.

As I descended toward the house, the veil shimmered into view. I flew through it, and as I entered, I shifted into my invisible skin, my death shade. Cloaked and hidden, I swooped through the window but misjudged my descent, disturbing a vase of flowers too close to the window. The vase crashed to the ground, announcing my arrival.

A stout woman with hair bound in a loose tapestry of graying braids atop her head rushed over to where I'd landed. "It's fine; it's just the wind," she called out. She huffed a little and tried to close the window, but it was stuck. "No time for this right now," she muttered as she scuttled out of the room.

I sniffed and examined her. She wasn't the one.

I took flight again, keeping low to the floor and maneuvering with some difficulty into the room with the blood and sweat, landing in the corner near the door. The older woman ignored me. A small woman with wet, curly hair plastered to her forehead stood on all fours on a pile of sheets and towels on the floor. She was naked from the waist down. Her legs were spread apart; she moaned, rocking back and forth. I recognized childbirth and, curious, moved in for a closer look.

The woman moaned again, grunting and gritting her teeth. She looked to be in extraordinary pain. The stout woman glided behind the laboring woman. "The baby's crowning," she said. "You're doing great, sweetheart. Keep pushing gently, breathe, that's it, we're *sooo* close, Carrie!"

Carrie took a deep breath, and for a moment, her body relaxed. Her hips rolled forward, and her back arched down, pulled by the weight of the child in her abdomen. With a soft shudder and a small sigh of relief, she looked up. She opened her mouth to speak when her gaze landed on me.

Which was, of course, impossible. She shouldn't have been able to see me. *Seeing me was absolutely not possible.*

But she did. Unaccountably. And at that moment, she and I both knew why I was there.

"Get out," she whispered, the blood draining from her face, leaving her skin pale and gray. "Motherfucker, get out! Get out! Get that fucking blackbird out of my house! Jake! Anna! GET IT OUT!"

Surprised by her outburst, the midwife sat back on her heels. "Honey, I need you to calm down," she cooed, trying to sound comforting. "Jake's not here, honey, he was called away to work. Don't worry; I'm not going anywhere. We're so close."

Carrie began her wailing again, and Anna, the midwife, began purring instructions even as she maneuvered between Carrie's shaking thighs. "All right, honey, the baby's head is out. Okay. Oh. Oh. Carrie, you have to push this baby out *now…*"

One minute, two minutes later, in a rush of blood and water, the baby slid between his mother's thighs and into the midwife's waiting hands. The tension in the air was palpable. I could have cut through it with a talon. The mother waited with bated breath, listening for the sound of her child's cry. The midwife worked her fingers at the child's airway, coaxing him to begin his mewling.

But it was not the air of trepidation that drew my attention to the child. It was the arrival of a new, bright, silver cord extending from beyond this world and attached to the child at the heel of his foot. And attached to the cord was a tag that read, "For Raven."

As soon as I'd seen the laboring woman, I'd known that I was here for her child. What I didn't know was which. Sometimes humans birth more than one, and it would be a real travesty were I to take the wrong soul. I must always wait for the tag with my name on it to glisten into view to show me which life I am to end.

This silver cord with its tell-tale name tag was bright and strong. It was my beacon, the next task on my to-do list. It sang in a quiet but brilliant frequency, and when I was confident that the child in the midwife's hands was my charge, I took flight, snapped the cord into my beak and slipped the soul from the freshly-born human baby.

As I flew with the cord securely in my mouth, I heard a woman's voice cry, "He's not breathing! Oh god, he's not breathing! Help, Anna, HE'S NOT BREATHING!"

I went out the same way her child came in: silent as the tomb.

Present Day

CARRIE IS STARING through me more than at me, as though she, too, is remembering the details of that day. "I never thought I'd see you again. Not much reason to, I guess, since I never carried to term again after that. Did you know that? I had four miscarriages before Mattie, and then you swooped in and carried him away. Just like," Carrie snapped her fingers. "That."

She looks different now, clothed and clean in the sunlight. Her hair is an explosion of bright, copper curls that reflect light like metal. If I were a magpie, I might try to capture some of that hair for a souvenir. But I know better than to get too close; she's wound so tight she's liable to do anything, and I don't want my life to end today.

This sentiment is shared by Andrew, who tries to gather his

sister into his arms. "Carrie, you're hysterical. Did you forget to take your meds? You know you have—"

"Would you just shut the fuck up?" she screams. On the other side of the line of trees, people are beginning to notice the commotion. Candace is hurrying over with the children at her heels; several other women are making similar headway. It's hard to tell if they genuinely want to help or are just nosey. With this crowd, one guess is as good as the other.

"I didn't forget to take my meds," she says with a sneer. "I'm just fucking *angry*, and that bird is the reason. You weren't there, so you don't know, but—"

Andrew's interruption is loud and frightening, even to me. "*Birds don't kill babies, Carrie!* Mattie didn't die because of any goddamn bird! Mattie died because you're sick, you weren't getting the help you needed, and you weren't able to take care of yourself! This doesn't have anything to do with that goddamn bird! You're deflecting again! And you're causing a goddamn scene."

Andrew's face is red, whether with embarrassment or frustration, I can't tell. Carrie is crying now, snot dripping from her nose. She ignores her brother and directs her next comments to me. "You know what I want from you? I want you to bring me another baby."

I cock my head to the side and blink. Now *that's* one I've never heard before. Storks bring babies to couples, not ravens. I hop a little closer to her. It isn't often that I am seen for what I am, and even more rarely that I am recognized for *who* I am. Carrie doesn't just see me for a raven; she knows we have met before. She knows I saw her naked and despairing. She knows I nabbed her child's life from this world. She knows me. She *sees* me.

And she *remembers* me. She shouldn't be able to. People almost universally don't recall the events that take place in the veil. But this woman sees me, she knows me, and she remembers. I am captivated. I cannot move away.

"You take lives all the time," she says, her voice breaking. "All I'm asking is that you bring me one of them. Instead of taking a soul away to wherever you take them, bring it to me. Put it in my womb. You can do that. You owe me, damn you."

Her tears fall freely, and I understand her pain, even if I hate her word choices. "Owe" is such a uniquely human word. It has no basis in reality.

"I carried that baby for nine months without even a hint of trouble," she whispers, her shoulders shaking. "It's not fair. You owe me."

"Fair" is right up there with "owe" as a word I have no use for. Andrew and Candace are flanking their sister now, one trying to calm her while the other berates her. The children look on, their worry and discomfort etched all over their faces. But no one seems to notice.

I take to the sky, putting distance between myself and the afternoon's strange events. Even if I wanted to help this woman, I can't. What do I know about bringing life to a womb? I don't even think it's possible. And where would I get a soul? It's not like extra souls are floating around, waiting to be snapped up and put to use. People are using the ones they have. That's the point. And the ones I take on the Virago's orders are accounted for, with family and friends waiting for them on the Other Side. It would be obvious if a dearly departed went missing. There's nothing I can do, and so I return to the treetops. But as I head away from the bedeviled family, I see something glittering in the dirt below me, and I swoop in to take a closer look.

CHAPTER THREE

IF I WERE DOWNTOWN instead of the middle of a park, I probably wouldn't have bothered. I learned years ago that what I thought was a diamond or peridot or even a plastic trinket is usually nothing more than a metal screw or a broken bicycle spoke or a shattered headlight. But out here, its shine cannot be ignored; it's so out of place amid the dirt and detritus from the trees that it catches my attention.

It's an earring.

I pull it up with my beak and examine it in the sunlight: it glitters like a gem, and though I know it isn't valuable in the human sense of the word—I've learned to identify glass and plastic by now, and this is undoubtedly the latter—I can't help but wonder if Magpie might like it. My heart flutters a bit at the thought of her, but I swallow the sentiment down. It's a silly emotion, and anyway, we are not birds of a feather. Still, we *are* friends, and I don't have anything better to do. I tuck the earring underneath my wing and set off in the direction of her nest.

You might not know it, but corvids are exceptionally intelligent. I don't say this to boast, but rather to set context. You might think all birds are the same, but it isn't true. Let's consider, for example, pigeons. Pigeons are the dumbest animals alive. You only have to look at the way they walk to see this for yourself: they shuffle their feet along the ground, picking up any manner of string and rubbish that gets attached to them. The string gets tangled around their feet and eventually cuts off their circulation, and before long, bits and pieces of their feet have rotted and fallen off. That's why pigeons are always in such dire straits: because they're too stupid or lazy to pick up their feet and walk properly.

Grackles, too, are monstrous, though not as stupid as pigeons. It's just that they're entirely self-centered and solipsistic, hardly ever stopping to consider the feelings of others. And Austin is plagued with them—and not the common grackle either, but those big sons of bitches, the great-tailed grackle. Countless times I've observed humans trying to take a nice lunch in the great out-of-doors only to be pushed inside by bellicose grackles who feel they are entitled to the french fries, tacos, even mayonnaise packets that you entertain yourselves with. They'll practically snatch the food right out of your hands if you're not careful. They're avian bullies, and if you ask me, a blight against the name of black birds everywhere. They aren't even corvids! Yet how many times have I been shooed away by a belligerent human shouting grackle-related insults at me? Too many. The existence of grackles mortally wounds me.

Magpies, however, are entirely different. First, they are corvids, like me, and that fact alone makes them respectable. Moreover, magpies have a reason for being. Just as I am a courier of death, magpies are collectors: they deal in treasure. If you ever need to locate a rare object or collect data about an obscure trinket, the magpies are your bird. Of course, this information isn't useful to humans. Most of us can't speak to you. So while you can ask a magpie where to find your misplaced engagement ring, and she can even tell you, you won't be able to understand.

The magpie with whom I have a delicate relationship lives on the far south end of Mary Moore Searight Park, almost where the park begins to peter out and turn into wilderness. It's peaceful out as I soar my way to her. I fly over groups of humans playing frisbee golf, the rules of which I have never been able to discern. When I arrive at the magpie's nest, I find her enjoying a breakfast of tomatoes and honeycomb she's undoubtedly nicked from a local farmer's market. In any case, I know the goods are ill-gotten, which makes them even more delectable. When she sees me, her eyes grow wide with joy, and she fluffs her wings and hops from foot to foot.

"Raven!" she exclaims with glee. "It's been such a long time since I've seen you. I'm glad to see that you're still willing to make my acquaintance. I'd begun to think you'd acquired a girlfriend in some other part of town, and you weren't interested in me anymore."

I know she's kidding, and I grin at the rib. We both know that in my line of work, taking on a love interest is irresponsible. Love is always fraught with the possibility of heartbreak, and after all these years of reaping, I don't have the wherewithal for it. My fortitude is lacking. My day job brings me enough grief as it is.

"I've brought you something," I say, reaching under my wing to retrieve the earring. I drop it on the tree branch in front of her and watch her eyes grow wide as she approaches. The faux emerald earring glistens in the sunlight, and I take particular delight in the awe that transforms the magpie's face into something celestial. That's the lovely thing about magpies. They don't actually care about things being real. They only care that things are beautiful.

"Where did you find this?" she asks, hardly daring to touch it. "I've been searching for something just like this for quite some time. Last week I managed to find some great bottle caps and even a metal sewing thimble, but I've never had anything as heavenly as this."

"I found it on the ground at Oktoberfest," I say almost dismissively. "God only knows why anybody would be wearing something like this to Oktoberfest, but, you know. It's Austin. Anyway, as soon as I saw it, I knew you had to have it. So here I am. Bearing gifts, as it were."

The magpie trills prettily in her excitement and finally bends down to lift the earring with her beak. She's so enchanted with the shine that she hardly remembers to thank me, but her reaction is all the thanks I need. "I can't wait to add this to my collection. It's perfect. You know, I knew you were coming today. I got extra fruit just for you," she says, nudging a bit of tomato my way. "I have a message for you from the Virago."

My heart sinks into my talons, and a gray grief passes over me. I should have known this was coming. I haven't had to kill anyone since the bride a few months back. I should have known my good fortune couldn't last forever; after all, it isn't like I get to retire. I'll have to endure this awful job until the day I die. Whenever the Virago sees fit for *that* to happen.

"Your business lies out near Todd Mission today," she says. "I know that's farther than you like to fly, but the good news is, your business is at the Renaissance Festival. So if you have to go all the way out there, at least your destination is a good one. You can stuff yourself on all the popcorn, cotton candy, and apples that your belly can hold." She giggles as she says this, and for a second, my spirits lift at the sound, but the moment passes quickly.

I sigh and give a small nod. It isn't the magpie's fault that I have a new assignment. "I'm sure there will be a cornucopia of snacks to feast on," I say with a false smile. The knowledge that I have to work today has utterly destroyed my appetite. "If you have to die, who *wouldn't* want to die in the great outdoors at the season's most festive event?"

The magpie nods her agreement; she's never had much of an ear for sarcasm. She's already searching for a place to store her new earring, somewhere she can admire its exceptional beauty; somewhere others will leer at it in jealousy. I do adore the magpie, but she's not exactly modest. It swells her head a bit when others look on her nest with envy.

Since she's no longer paying attention to me and my self-pity has already reached insufferable levels, I forgo the formality of saying goodbye. I take to the air to begin the long flight to Todd Mission, a grim resignation in the pit of my soul. I look back only once and only for a moment, hoping to see her eyes follow the trail of my flight, to feel her gaze like sun rays on my feathers. But the magpie is not watching me. Once again, I'm alone.

If you've never been to the Texas Renaissance Festival, I can't recommend it enough, even though many have suggested it's not a Renaissance Festival in the truest sense of the term. It's more of a pleasure fair. Almost no one dresses in historical clothing, although when you think about it, the weather in Texas is not at all suitable to the kind of clothing humans would have worn back in pre-global warming England where it was cold and wet a good majority of the time. So perhaps it's appropriate that the outfits of the Texas Renaissance Festival more closely resemble something you might find in a comic book. Fairies with gossamer wings, tall, furry humanoid creatures from a popular space opera franchise, all manner of pirates, gypsies, and ladies scantily clad in something that is supposed to resemble ring armor. It's a delightful display of flesh and fancy.

By the time I make it all the way out to Todd Mission, Texas, I'm ravenous. I feel as though I could eat a whole hog. The primary food stations are full of delectable treats: banana empanadas, Scotch eggs, loaded baked potatoes, and more tie my stomach up in knots. I know better than to try to eat here near the entrance, however, unless I want to be crushed underfoot by throngs of drunkards. I'm looking for something with a little bit more privacy, so I head to the fair's far edge where the crowds are thinner and the food just as tasty.

It isn't long before I see what I'm in the mood for. A family of four is just finishing up their lunch of turkey legs, funnel cake, and what appears to be apple fritters. Just as the family is disentangling themselves from the picnic table and about to dump their food into the garbage, I swoop down close enough to startle them. The mother looks at me and frowns, ushering her children away. Her skins crawls just to look at me.

I wait for the family to disappear before I hop over to their leavings. It's everything I hoped it would be. I gorge myself on turkey leg and desserts and am about to begin my day's investigations when I hear a familiar noise.

Just up ahead, an embarrassment of grackles has spied my feast. I can already tell they're making plans to come over here and reap their rewards. I haven't finished everything, and my belly is full, but I can't stomach the idea of giving grackles any leeway. Give those bastards an inch, and they'll take a mile.

I don't want the Renaissance Festival to become a breeding ground for bastards. So I make my wings as big as I can, lean my head back, and open up my beak to let out a series of spine-tingling croaks.

It has the desired effect, sending the grackles screaming into the air, flying away from the territory I've claimed. I chuckle at their quick departure, their spineless whinnying, their ignoble cowardice. Grackles are all bark and no bite.

My hunger and bravado sated, I suppose I can't put off the inevitable any longer. I take to the sky languidly, keeping my eyes on the silver cords that wind their way to heaven. One of these people is going to die today, though I have no idea who. Would it be so hard for the magpie to give me more of a hint? *Oh, it'll be a balding woman with a limp who will slice the throat of an ex-lover in a brawl!* Or perhaps, *Be on the lookout for a gang of angsty teenagers who will accidentally shoot an arrow into a pirate's good eye!* But no, all I ever hear is, "Head to this location. Await further orders."

It's a dismal job. If I had known this as a young raven, would I still have heeded the call?

As I'm feeling sorry for myself, I look down to see a crowd beginning to gather at one of the larger, open-air stages. A lot more people are coming, and despite myself, I find excitement blooming in my belly. I may be a raven, but I enjoy a good show as much as anyone. I've seen men eat fire, women who levitate, and dancers who could practically dislocate their hips from the rest of their bodies. I've seen a bald man dance with a whip made of fire, a ventriloquist tell lewd jokes by way of his skeletal puppet, and fat, bawdy women casting ghastly aspersions at passers-by in the hopes of riling them up enough to get them to spend their hard-earned cash on dunking the villainous wenches in cold water.

So while I don't know what kind of show this will be, I am intrigued. This many comers can't be wrong.

I find a comfortable spot perched in a nearby tree. The benches below have begun to fill in, and the local snack merchants have likewise descended, hawking candied popcorn and pretzels and beer. They wander up and down the aisles, trading food for bills as children scream, fathers dab their balding heads with baseball caps, and mothers sigh as they wipe buttery smudges from their children's mouths.

As I'm settling in, I hear someone down below shouting. "Arnold! The hell are you doing up there? Get down here where you belong. The show's about to start!"

The shouting voice carries an affected Elizabethan English accent, so I know whoever it is must be part of the show. I crane my neck over the crowd, looking for the shouter and the offending Arnold. I find the shouter pounding his way down the aisle, his ruffled cotton shirt slipping down a sunburnt shoulder. He is in bad need of a shave, and his cheeks are red and chapped. He looks up at me and calls again. "Arnold! I know you hear me talking to you! Get down here right now, ye right cretin, and you'll get yourself a nice tasty treat if'n ya do."

I'm momentarily confounded as to why this man is yelling at me until I notice the most important thing about him: he's wearing a falconer's glove on his left hand. I suck in a breath and take a look around, feeling stupid that I hadn't noticed it immediately. This isn't any stage: it's the falconer's stage. And that fellow shouting at me from the ground has mistaken me for one of his birds.

Now, I've never had any particular desire to be an entertainer. I've always been quite happy to watch humans, not perform for them. But he's waiting for me, and now the crowd is waiting as well. And so, uncharacteristically, I humor him. I fly from my perch to land elegantly on the chap's hand. The crowd claps politely. The man shakes his head at me and says in a scolding voice, "I don't even know how you got out of your cage. I'll have to talk to Amanda about that later. Means she's been slacking on the job again. Probably been fooling around with that boy from the chain mail shop." His brow wrinkles as he catches sight of my white feathers and says, "Ye've got makeup on your cheek. You been snogging with some whitefaced harlot?"

The crowd titters, and a child stage-whispers, "What's a harlot?" and the laughter grows louder.

I arch my chest a bit and throw my head back, making my feathers appear as fluffy and glossy and impressive as possible. The man shakes his head as he climbs onto the stage, holding me close to his chest. Once he's in position, he begins to speak to the crowd.

"You're all about to see what it takes to train a raven such as this," he says, his voice booming over the crowd. "Ravens, as you may know, are the most intelligent birds in North America. And I've trained this one to perform a series of tricks which I purport to share with you today."

The crowd's eyes are on the stage in such rapt attention

that for a moment, I forget that I'm supposed to be on a mission of death. I'm *excited* to be part of the show, but at the same time, I don't know what kind of choreography I will be expected to perform. What if he tries to shoot an apple off my head? Or what if I am supposed to sing a song, the notes of which I do not know? Not that *that* would be such a great travesty; ravens are wonderful dancers and proud mimics, but we're no great shakes in the music department. Nevertheless, I decide not to let stage fright get the better of me. Improv, they say, is a skill improved with practice. I don't know if that's true, but I guess we are about to find out.

The man raises me a foot or so above his head and looks me dead in the eye. "What tricks've ye got up your sleeve today, Arnold?" he asks. I fluff my feathers and shake my head as if to say I don't know. The audience chuckles. A few children squeal with delight. I redouble my efforts at amusement and hop a perfect 360 degrees on his hand. The falconer tsks at me, wagging a finger in my face, which I pretend to nip. He jerks his hand back and shakes his fingers to great laughter, now donning a frown that I know is for the audience, not me.

I feel *alive*.

"All right, Arnold. This is supposed to be *my* show. Stop stealing my limelight!" he says with a laugh. "All right. Let's see how good you are at Simon Says. Would you like that?"

He directs this question to the crowd, who bursts into applause in response. Pleased, the man nods and faces me. He clears his throat. "Simon says, hold out your left wing."

After pausing only for a moment, I do as the man has instructed, stretching my left wing as high and as far out as I can, ensuring that each feather is distinct from the others so that the audience can see how delightful and large and glorious my wing is. The audience laughs and claps, and I notice one man in particular near the front seems especially amused. He's a big man, wearing a court jester's hat and boasting a large, unruly white beard. He looks quite jolly, like a medieval Santa

Claus, and so I use him as my barometer. His laughter will indicate my success.

"All right, Arnold. That was pretty good, I guess. What I want to know now is: can you show us your left foot?"

I think about this for a moment, wondering what the man expects me to do. Eventually, I lift my left foot and extend it out to the audience as best I can. The audience breathes in sharply as the man waggles a finger in my face. "Arnold! I didn't say Simon says!"

The crowd moans their disappointment, and in response, I duck my head into my wing, feigning embarrassment. The crowd breaks into fresh laughter and rippling applause. The jolly man in the front row swipes at his forehead and chuckles, slapping his knee with his free hand. I'm on target, then. The audience is captivated.

"I got you fair and square on that one, Arnold. Let's try again. Simon says, extend your right wing *and* stick out your left foot."

Balancing precariously on my one foot, I extend my left leg and right wing, stretching them in opposite directions as dexterously and magnificently as I can. Then, just because the mood has gripped me, I lean my head back and open my beak as wide as I can and let out a mighty croak.

The crowd erupts into wild applause, punctuated by laughs, whistles, and shouts. The falconer seems pleased as well, and he pulls a snack out of his pocket and tries to feed it to me. It's not anything nearly as delicious as the turkey leg I had only moments ago, and I'm still stuffed to the crown, but to make him happy, I eat the treats. They're nothing more than peanuts; pretty bland fodder for someone like me. But I make a big show of eating them, tossing the peanuts up into the air before opening my beak wide and letting the nuts fall into my mouth. The crowd claps again. It seems everything I do wins their approval.

What a feeling!

But just as the falconer opens his mouth to offer me a new string of suggestions to amuse the crowd, I catch a glimpse of the jolly fellow in the front row. He's begun to sweat and has removed his jester hat to swipe his bald head with the palm of his hand. And as he does so, my heart stops.

No. Please, no. Not my muse.

I hadn't noticed it before, so taken I was with the positive attention I was receiving. But now that I'm looking, I can see that the veil has descended, shifting and shimmering, cocooning him in an undulating bubble made of light that renders him soft and fuzzy. With his hat now removed, I cannot deny what is right before my eyes. Clear as day, the glittering tag attached to his astral cord with my name on it flutters in the sparse breeze.

He's the one.

Taking a deep breath, I lift my eyes skyward and curse my fate. Why this man? And why now? And why me? Is this fellow a good man? Is he beloved? Or is he someone the world will be better off without? I can't possibly know, and what's more, it doesn't matter. My job is the same no matter who he is. No amount of goodness or charity or righteousness can buttress us against our fate.

Death is not discriminating. It comes for us all.

I launch myself from the falconer's glove and the audience oohs and ahhhs at my agility, but they are especially surprised when I swoop down towards the man in the front row. Of course, they don't know what's happening: his cord is not visible to the human eye. It's only visible to reapers like me. Usually, I would slip into my invisible skin before initiating my attack, but under these circumstances, preening like a fool before a crowd of humans, it would be more jarring to disappear when all eyes are on me. Instead, I close my eyes, every bit of me nakedly visible as I snap his cord into my beak and lift gently, easing his soul from his body.

Gasps and shouts take up the space I leave in my wake. I

glance back to see that the man has toppled over, thick hands clutching at his throat as he crumbles into the dirt, the jester hat lying forgotten on the bench where he once sat. A few faces turn my way as the falconer shouts for me to return and stage-hands run amok, shouting to the falconer and shaking their heads in dismay.

I imagine them explaining to a befuddled falconer that I am not Arnold. Only after the paramedics have come and gone, carrying my muse away on a gurney, will they run backstage to find Arnold sitting in his cage, waiting to be fed peanuts in exchange for silly tricks for humans who will laugh and clap and chant his name. As I think on him, my heart grows heavy with the spirit of envy.

I *envy* Arnold. Arnold, who lives in a cage. Arnold, whose days are carefully scripted and measured, decided before he even hatched from his egg. Arnold, who never eats turkey legs or funnel cakes and who has no Magpie to lavish with treasure.

But also Arnold, who brings such joy. Arnold, who is beloved and never scorned. Arnold, whose existence earns whispers of love and affection. Arnold, who soars into cheers and applause and knows nothing of the mournful wails that beleaguer my working hours.

Arnold has only half the freedom I have. And yet, what a joy it must be to be Arnold.

I want to be Arnold.

As I soar higher into the sky with the cord in my beak, my heart feels heavier than usual. It's not because I am upset about the work I've performed: this man's death is just one of so many under my wing. No, this heaviness is different. As I stood on that stage, performing small tricks and making people smile and laugh, I felt something unfurl inside me that I'd never experienced before. I am accustomed to leaving hysteria and desolation in my wake. But never before have I elicited such warmth and affection from humans.

That feeling was delicious. And I want more of it.

As I kite the jester's soul behind me, a recent memory flickers into my mind, and I find myself thinking of Carrie — the woman in the park who asked me to bring her a baby. I recall the expression on her face, the desperation in her eyes. If I were to bring her a child, wouldn't that pain be replaced with absolute joy? Wouldn't she think me the most glorious creature in all the universe?

If I can make an audience of people laugh and clap and shout for me because I raised my leg and stretched out my wing on command, wouldn't that woman Carrie think me a *god* for bringing her a child?

Is it possible…?

The tactical process itself is the problem. A soul marked for death is easy to transport; the veil appears, and I pass into to it to take the life, and I pass out of it to carry the soul to the Other Side. But those souls are accounted for; they have people waiting for them, including the Virago. I couldn't merely kidnap one for my own purposes.

What I need is a soul *not* marked for death. A soul no one would be looking for. And then I need a way to carry it to the Other Side, but the veil only appears at the appointed time of death. And even if I solve this problem, rebirthing it is utterly beyond my ken. Contrary to popular belief, there's no such thing as reincarnation. Once a soul has passed over to the Far Shore, he's unfit for corporeal confinement; the body rejects it.

So for this to work, I'd have to take a new soul. A soul freshly dead that has not passed over to the Far Shore. A soul unaccompanied by a reaper and with no friends or family awaiting him.

And the only way to do that would be to reap a soul from Earth myself. But then there's the problem of transporting it without a veil, not to mention the logistics of getting it where it needs to go without being noticed.

It's impossible. As much as I want to help Carrie, there's just no way to do it.

A squeal of laughter below me catches my attention. I glance down to see two children dressed as matching clowns pointing skyward, the paint on their twin white faces smudged.

And then it hits me.

It's nearly Halloween. All Hallows' eve. Eve of All Saints. My heart begins to beat loudly in my ears as I realize that for one night, all of Austin will be shrouded in the veil as the souls who have passed on are allowed to come back and visit the relatives they've left behind. There will be so much traffic moving from one place to another that no one will notice a stray soul being hand-delivered into a place it was never intended for. Halloween night is always something of a shit-show. But that could work to my advantage.

If I architect it correctly, it's possible. It's the only night of the year that it is.

The plan is rough and needs refinement. There's so much I don't know. But as the possibility grows in my heart, I feel a giddiness I haven't felt since I was a young reaper recruit.

I'm going to bring Carrie a baby.

But I won't bring her just any soul. If I'm going to do this, I only get one shot. I need to bring her the *right* soul. Someone who will be a joy to Carrie for the rest of her life. Someone who will light up her life and love her with their full heart. Someone who will enter into their new life with utter gusto. Which means I can't just nab any random soul from the street. I need to *choose* my gift.

I have no idea how to execute such a plan. It's so danger-ous, and anything could go wrong. What if I'm caught? What if I kill them successfully but can't figure out how to bring them back? My head is full of questions, and I have not a single answer. But now that the idea has taken root, I know I can't turn back. And so I, a raven, a bringer of death, will now embark on a new journey: to find the right soul to take for beautiful, sad, damaged Carrie.

I've never been more excited in my life.

CHAPTER FOUR

October 17th

MORNING ROLLS OVER THE hill country with its usual languor, and light rain is beginning to fall. The drizzle feels like a dream, and I stretch my wings and blink my eyes to wake myself up. A thin fog is collecting along the ground, and the smell of ozone and petrichor tickle my nostrils. Rain is my favorite weather. It drapes the world in watercolor, and everything feels slightly less real. Perhaps that's just my inner romantic talking, but I find it so much easier to perform my work against a background of a water-logged sky and soft, soggy ground.

My stomach rumbles. Mornings like this are no good for scavenging food from humans at local cafés; the rain will keep them indoors with their bagels and hot coffee and crispy bacon. Breakfast for me will be something healthful then, like tomato or acorn. I wonder if the magpie —

A rustling of nearby leaves interrupts my thoughts, and I swivel my head around quickly to see that for once, I am not alone.

A strange raven is sitting on a branch next to me, watching

me with an expression that could be contemplation or could be plotting. As in, he could be contemplating the meaning of life, or he could be plotting to murder me in my sleep. Except I'm not asleep anymore, and this raven looks rather young—too young, probably, to be considering something as emo as murder first thing in the morning.

He doesn't speak, just stands there, quietly watching me. The creepiness of his silence gives me the goosebumps. Only psychopaths watch other people sleep. Well, psychopaths and parents, I suppose, though the line there is a bit thin. "Can I help you?" I ask finally, my feathers ruffled.

The raven moves in closer and opens his beak in an approximation of a smile. He puffs out his chest and stamps his feet excitedly. "I've been waiting for you to wake up for the better part of an hour," he says.

I blink and frown. "That long? Sorry to keep you. I didn't know I was on a schedule." He takes the admonishment well, having the decency to drop his eyes as I say, "Is there something I can help you with?"

The young raven looks up now and clears his throat. Any bravado he had a moment ago is gone, replaced by nervousness. Before the words are even out of his mouth, my heart sinks into my feet. There's only one reason a young bird would be at my nest this early on a rainy morning. "The Virago sent me. I'm starting my reaper training today, and she assigned me to you. I'm your new apprentice, reporting for duty."

I clamp my beak shut to contain the moan that's trying to escape. Somewhere in the back of mind, I guess I've been anticipating this moment. After all, I once had a mentor—in fact, I've been unlucky enough to have several. But maybe part of me hoped that the Virago would think me too important, too busy, too *something* to be burdened with an apprentice of my own.

When I'm sure I won't say something I'll later regret, I

open my beak. "Is this your first job, or are you being reassigned?"

The young reaper stands a little straighter as he says, "This is my first job, sir."

Well, that's good, at least. Means I'm not inheriting someone else's problem. I look him over from head to talon. He looks healthy and robust. His feathers are well kept, his beak shiny and sharp, the eyes bright and curious. His feet look healthy—no signs of rot, and the talons look like they could pierce metal. As ravens go, this one is a fine specimen. It could be worse: A raven I used to fly with long ago was once saddled for two weeks with a cross-eyed bird who stuttered and favored his left wing, so if he wasn't careful, he'd fly to the right instead of in a straight line, which would eventually take him in a great circle. He didn't last long.

"I suppose you've brought a letter of commendation?"

My new apprentice retrieves a bit of paper from underneath a wing and hands it to me. I take it and drop it into my nest. I'll read it later, or I won't. It doesn't matter what the letter says; I just wanted to be sure he had one. Because that means the Virago really, truly did send him.

And that means trouble for me.

"So!" I don a false smile. "Tell me something about yourself."

My apprentice heaves a relieved sigh and launches into a story that I'm not listening to and don't care about. I need him to talk while I think.

Halloween is in two weeks. I have fourteen days to canvas the city and find the right mark. That's a tight timeline under the best circumstances: you can't usually get a good bead on someone without getting to know them for a while. In my case, since I can't exactly get to know these humans, I'll have to follow them. Watch them in their natural habitat. That means surveillance, which takes time.

And it also means privacy. Which, thanks to the prattling nincompoop standing before me, I no longer have.

Dammit, Virago! I curse, shaking my head in frustration. *How am I supposed to succeed in this mission with a yapping adolescent shadowing me everywhere I go?*

But he's not my only problem. An apprentice means work. Active deaths. Which means I won't *have* the leisure time to tail and surveil humans. I'll be too busy reaping so this whipper-snapper can learn the ins and outs of the game.

It's the most rotten luck I can think of, and my frustration must show on my face because the apprentice cocks his head at me, his face feathers dropping into a frown. "Something the matter? Are you okay, sir? Can I get you something?"

I feign a smile. "I'm fine. I just wasn't expecting you. Just throws a bit of a wrench in my day." Which is the understatement of the year.

The young bird nods as though he understands. "Ah, I see. Well, I guess that explains why you were asleep when I got here. I was expecting a warmer welcome." His subtle chastisement is not lost on me, but I don't bristle. I can hold my tongue with the best of them. "At any rate, the Virago sent me with a message also."

I sigh and hang my head. A message. No rest for the wicked, then. She means for us to get started right away. "All right; what's the message?"

The young bird cocks his head to the side and squints his eyes at me. "Don't you want to know my name first?"

I almost laugh but catch myself just in time. "Mentors rarely use names with their apprentices," I say. "The tradition is to use a nickname, which you'll earn once I get to know you better. In the meantime, you're just Apprentice." I don't say this with any malice, but my voice isn't exactly dripping with honey, either. "So. You have a message for me?"

"For *us*," he corrects self-importantly. "The Virago says to go to the dilapidated gray house three rows west of the Kwik-

Stop-Shop on the other side of the highway. She called it the Duval house. You know it?"

I shrug. "I know the area she means. I'm sure the house will be apparent when we get there. Anything else?"

My apprentice nods. "She says she's done all she can, but it's a kidnap job." He stamps his feet and ruffles his wings. "What's a kidnap job?"

The words ripple through me until my blood runs cold. Goose pimples form underneath my feathers, and I'm thankful for my lofty plumage so that this newcomer can't see my distress. "She literally means the person we're reaping today was forcibly taken against their will. Which has implications for us." I lay the scenario out as plainly as I can. "One, the person we have to reap is sealed away with no easy access to them. The Virago usually clears our path—opens windows, leaves doors ajar, coaxes people into open spaces. Then, at the appointed time of death, the veil shimmers into view, and we go through. But in a kidnap situation, there's usually no easy way in."

The young bird looks at me quizzically, and his expression reminds me that he has no idea what I'm talking about. He's never been on a reap before; he doesn't even understand the fundamentals of the job. "The veil?"

I curse inwardly again, my blood pressure rising. Why has the Virago chosen to send us on a kidnap mission? If I'm to train him, shouldn't we start with something basic? Something simple? The surprise deaths are the easiest. Yeah, they're the most tragic for those left behind, but for the one reaping? Easy as pie. You dive in, nip the cord, the person drops dead, you head home.

So why a kidnap job? Certainly, other reapers could have handled this today.

"The veil is what separates the world of the living and the world of the dead—the Great Beyond, the Other Side, whatever you want to call it. It doesn't look like much—it's just a bubble of energy. But anyway, it encompasses the person who's about to die. Sometimes the veil is big—the size of the whole house or building. Sometimes it's the size of a small room. Everything inside the veil feels surreal. Like a dream. We call it veil sickness. Anyway, when reapers go through it from this side, we can shift skin—become invisible. Which is why it's nice when the veil is big, because we can shift skin sooner. Then, once we have the mark, we fly out. This part's important: you have to pierce the veil with your beak and then fly through. That's why we're so important; humans can't do it on their own. That's the only way to get to the Other Side."

Apprentice has hardly blinked as I've described the mechanics of our job. I remember my mentor explaining to me how it works—well, trying to explain. He'd been drunk at the time. Apprentice rubs his feathers together and lifts a wing. "Ah, a question? How do we know which soul is ours to take?"

"You know about the glittering silver cord?"

Apprentice nods. "It's what connects the soul and the body."

I think about this a second. "Close, but no cigar. It's what connects the soul to the Other Side. The soul slips inside a body some time before birth, and it'll stay there until one of us takes it away. But that soul is anchored to the Great Beyond by a glittering silver cord. Our job is to grab the cord, lift the accompanying soul out of the body, and take it back. Like lifting a tea bag out of water."

I grin at my apt description, but my apprentice looks like he doesn't drink tea. "Anyway, to answer your question, to know which soul is your mark, you need to look for your name tag on it."

The young bird steps closer to me, eyes round as oranges. "My name?"

"Yes. In a room full of people, you know your soul by the name tag. And if several people are dying, you need to know which soul is yours. Sometimes there will be competition, you see. You're not the only reaper in the area. If many people are dying, you aren't likely to be able to take them all. More importantly, you don't want to take the *wrong* soul. Ever. That's the worst thing we can do as reapers—take a soul that isn't marked for reaping. Life is too precious."

The bird throws a quizzical glance my way, head cocked to the side. "Life is precious? What a strange thing for you to say. I thought that, being in the business of death as we are, you would say that *death* is precious."

I stamp my foot in irritation and fluff my feathers. "Death is inevitable," I say with a scowl. "There's nothing sacred or interesting in it. Everyone who lives will die. But life? Life is a mystery. No one knows how it began, how it started. *Why* are we alive? For what purpose? To what end? Life is fraught with questions like these. Death is paltry in comparison."

I know this isn't what I should say to him. As his mentor, I'm supposed to build him up, make him proud of the work. More than merely teaching him the ins and outs of the job, I'm supposed to teach him the philosophy of the reap. I'm supposed to explain that our job is to provide continuity between the stages of existence. I'm supposed to tell him that death is both an end and a new beginning. I'm supposed to explain that as psychopomps, our highest duty is to guard the soul through transition, preparing it to become part and parcel of the universe once more.

But I'm not the bird to tell him these things, because I no longer believe them myself. Death is a dirty, horrible business. It brings nothing but pain and misery.

The young bird sighs and shakes his head. "Uh, okay. If you say so, I guess I'll take your word for it."

I lift an eyebrow. "How magnanimous of you. The only thing you have to understand today is the fundamentals of a reap. You have to look for the shining silver astral cord with your name—or, today it'll probably be my name—on it. Don't do anything until you see the tag. Do you understand?"

The fellow gives a slow nod as he takes in this information. "In summary," the smaller raven drawls, thoughtfully tapping his beak with the tip of his wing, "my first order of business is to locate my mark. Once the veil appears, I go in and turn invisible. Then I look for a tag on the glittering silver cord with my name on it. If it has my name on it, I take it and carry it up to the Great Beyond. But if it doesn't have my name on it, I'm to leave it alone. Even if it has another raven's name on it. Is that it?"

"That's the gist," I say. "The most important thing for today is that you must do exactly as I tell you, no matter what." I give him a sharp look and take a few steps toward him. To his credit, he doesn't back away. "If I tell you to jump, you do it. If I tell you to run, you do it. If I tell you to pluck out your own eyes, you do it. I don't want any acts of bravado. Anything can happen on one of these kidnap calls. So keep your wits about you, and do exactly as I say. And watch your back. Let's go."

I take to the sky, and the apprentice follows close behind. When we get close, I sink lower into the sky to assess the area. I see the Kiwk-Stop-Shop and count the rows until I see the little dilapidated gray house where our job today lies. There are front and back yards, a porch, and a rusted-out truck in the driveway. Most of the windows are covered in grime, and the others are boarded up. There are no chimneys, and because of the porch roof, I can't see the condition of the front door. From the outside, it doesn't even look like anyone lives there.

Shit.

I take a sharp dive and careen to the left, away from the house and our destination. We land a few dirt roads away from our target house. When my apprentice gets close enough, I explain the situation. "I've got a bad feeling about this."

My apprentice raises an eyebrow. "Bad feeling how?"

I shake my head. "I don't know. I just…you gotta stay close and pay attention. Getting into that house is gonna be tricky. Did you see a way in?"

My apprentice shakes his head. "All the windows were closed up tight."

I nod, impressed with his observation. "Yeah. Plus, we know we're here on a kidnapping, so we're not dealing with entirely sane people. So just...I don't know, just be careful. Let's go."

We launch ourselves into the sky and make our way toward the Duval house. We do not fly directly to it; instead, we err on the side of caution, making a wide circle around the house, searching once more for points of entry. I think there might be a small hole in the roof, or maybe —

A bullet zings by, so close that the air around me vibrates and I career off course. I cry out to alert my apprentice, but he's already changing direction. I look down, trying to see where the shot came from. A man stands in the front yard with a rifle, retargeting me. I suck in a breath and pull my wings close, hoping to outmaneuver the shooter.

BOOM.

I cry out again because I can't see my apprentice. I can't tell if that bullet was meant for him or me, but I have a terrible feeling that at any moment now, he's going to pull that trigger again, and —

BOOM. The shockwaves resonate through my body as the bullet clips me in my left wing. I screech with surprise and fear and begin to fall. I glance wingward to see how hurt I am, but I don't see any blood. The bullet didn't hit me in the meat of my wing; he's only clipped my coverts. By the time I right myself and reorient to the scene, I see my apprentice flying around to the back of the house.

"This way!" he calls out.

Dazed and overblown with adrenaline, I follow the sound of my apprentice's voice to the rear of the house. The shooting seems to have stopped. We land in a patch of brown grass to catch our breath. My apprentice's eyes are wild with fear.

"Are you okay?" I ask, glancing at my torn feathers trailing the ground. "Did you —"

"Look."

I turn to follow my apprentice's gaze. Lined up at the back of the house is a row of rusty birdcages, all facing the same direction. Whether it's morbid curiosity or a sense of duty, I don't know, but something pulls us toward those cages even though my intuition is howling at me to get away from this place. It's only when we're close enough to smell the remains that we see the true horror.

Inside each cage is a dead raven. And each raven's wings have been ripped from his body.

"JESUS CHRIST, what kind of people are we dealing with?"

My apprentice's words echo my thoughts, but I have no reply. The day's urgency has suddenly skyrocketed. "We need to get inside that house and find our mark as fast as we can. I don't want to end up like that."

Keeping low to the ground, we investigate the back of the house. The windows are tightly shut. There is no back door. There is no cellar that I can see, and no chimney to sweep down. Still, there must be a way inside without going out front where we're sure to be shot on sight. The Virago always provides passage. She doesn't always make it obvious, though.

"I don't like this," he says. "I don't know what we're supposed to be doing here. Maybe I misunderstood. Maybe this isn't the right house. Maybe —"

"This is the right house," I say, my eyes moving carefully over the premises. "It's just like this sometimes. I had a reap once where —"

Mid-thought, I see something out of place. By the back door is a large shed attached to the house. The shed's door is locked shut, so I had already dismissed it as a way into the house. But just now, my eyes catch a bit of movement. I see the bushy black tail of a rock squirrel burrowing into a rodent-sized tunnel underneath the shed. And then I gasp.

"I got it," I say, keeping my voice low. "There. Under the shed. The rock squirrels have dug a burrow. I bet it goes underneath the house. We might be able to squeeze through and up into the floorboards. And if we get lucky..."

We make our way to the shed, hot on the squirrel's paws. The hole is tighter than I like, but we don't seem to have any alternatives. I crouch low, pressing my chest against the ground and wriggling my way through the opening. Apprentice is so close behind that I feel his breath on my tail feathers. We inch forward, making slow progress. The tunnel is so narrow that our bodies scrape against the sides.

Past the point of no return, I heave a deep sigh, letting my breath out in a whoosh. I can hear the rock squirrel up ahead, and I hope that means that the tunnel will widen. If the creature has made a nest down here, perhaps that means babies. And babies mean more space. I hope.

We're a few feet further in, and finally, it happens. The space opens up, and the feel of the tunnel changes. There's no cement above us now; it's wood. I sigh with tremendous relief that we must be beneath the house.

I beckon with a roll of my head for the apprentice to follow me. "We need to find a loose floorboard or some entry point into the house. We'll have to tap the wood with our beaks to look for weak points. Whatever you do, keep as quiet as possible. I don't need to remind you what these people might do if they find us."

Creeping around under the house is terrifying. I didn't know I was claustrophobic, but turns out, I am. Christ. Poking our beaks up at the floorboards, we look for weaknesses; nails that have come loose, rotten wood that we can pry apart. It takes a lot longer than I expected. Ten or fifteen minutes in, I'm sweating like a dog, and my apprentice is beginning to whine and mutter to himself. He's irritating my already-shot nerves, and if I don't get out of here soon, I'm going to kill more than just my mark.

Finally, I feel something give. I halt and beckon for the apprentice to do the same. "Come here," I say. "Right here. There's a loose board. If you help me, we can probably get it loose enough to wiggle through."

Apprentice nods, but he has fear in his eyes. "What do we do if our guy's up there and he sees us first? I don't want to end up like those ravens outside."

I shake my head. "We won't. I can almost guarantee our mark isn't the one who did that; that was the psychopath who shot at us. Still, stay sharp. No telling what we're about to walk into."

Apprentice is shaking, and I step close enough to him to nudge him with my head. It's as close to kindness as I can muster under these circumstances. "You'll be okay," I say. "You can do this. I know this is a hell of a first mission, but think of it this way; you'll have conquered possibly the hardest reap you'll ever have to do."

This does little to calm him, but he swallows and nods just the same. "Right there," I say, indicating a spot on the wooden slats above us. "Press right there, and I think we can get inside. Ready? One, two…"

Our heads pop through the floor before I get to three. I struggle through first. We're in the kitchen; it looks like no one has used it in ages. The air smells sweetly stale and organic, like something rotting. There's no air conditioning, and the room is sweltering. I fly up to a countertop to get a better look.

"I think we might be able to get into the walls from here," I say. "Look over there." I indicate an air duct covering hanging from the ceiling by a single screw; the other is missing. "I think we can knock the grating down and get inside. From there, we should have access to the whole house."

Apprentice nods and stamps his feet. "Just tell me what to do," he says. "I'm ready."

I fly up to the grating and catch the loose corner under my beak. I press down, but it doesn't come undone. I try again with the same result.

"Use your talons," my apprentice says. "I think if you hang from it with all your weight, it might come off."

I grunt and reach my talons underneath the metal. Then, folding my wings into my body, I allow myself to give in to gravity.

My full weight tugging on the grating does the trick, and the metal clatters to the floor. I grimace at the ruckus, sure that someone must have heard the noise.

I fly up into the duct. The clack of our talons on metal echoes throughout and I grit my mandibles. We take one turn and then another until at last, we come to a hole with no grating on the other side.

Thank you, Virago.

"Here we go," I say. "I'll go first. Like I said before, be ready for anything. You good?"

Apprentice nods.

We descend into the room, and a bodily stench fills our nostrils. It's human—body odor, feces, urine. The stink is so overpowering I almost don't notice the next smell: blood.

A young man is sitting with his back against a wall, legs splayed out before him. He's completely naked. What hair he has left hangs in matted tangles in front of a broken face. His nails are caked with dirt or blood; I can't tell which. Circular burn marks run up and down his calves. Some are almost healed; others look brand new. His arms, rail thin and the skin nearly translucent, rest lightly on his thighs, great streams of thick, purple blood draining from his sliced veins, pooling in sickening puddles beneath his legs. At the sight of him, I cry out and retch. The veil hasn't appeared yet; everything is still sharp and clear. And yet there's no doubt in my mind this is the right mark.

A shattered dinner plate lies next to the young man, and

one particularly long, sharp piece sits just underneath him, its pointed tip red with gore. He must have used this shard to slice the veins. He's done it right, too, slicing the length of his arm from crook to wrist. It can't have been easy; the shard is sharp but ragged and uneven. The fissure down his arm is jagged, deep, and erratic like a perverse Mississippi River.

"Jesus Christ," I whisper, my heart pounding in my ears. "Jesus Christ, what happened to him? Who did this to him?"

My apprentice frowns as he waddles close to the blood. "That's pretty obvious. The same person who got those ravens. Probably the same person who tried to shoot us down."

I look at the young man. He can't be more than twenty, his face speckled with acne. He has almost no facial hair. His breathing is shallow. He's staring right at me, eyes alert and unblinking, and because there's no veil, I haven't shifted skin. He sees me, but there's no fear or confusion or any other emotion in those eyes. It's like he's empty, his essence run out with all the blood.

"Why did she send *us*?" I whisper to no one in particular. "She could have sent someone to help this kid! Shit, there's no veil, so maybe there's time! Maybe she doesn't want us to reap him at all; maybe she wants us to bring help—"

"He wants to die," my apprentice interrupts, his voice flat and even. "Doesn't take a genius to see that. By the looks of him, he's been held here for a long time. A *long* time. Look at that door. It's like the door of a safe. How do you propose to get someone past that?" He shakes his head. "Nah, this kid's toast. Nobody's coming for him. Let's reap him and go," he says.

"There has to be something we can do!" I cry. The young man's eyes continue to follow me as I pace, waiting for the veil, my breathing coming harder and faster. "People aren't supposed to die like animals in cages, like—"

"Like those ravens?"

His voice is cold when it cuts through the darkness. "You

care a helluva lot more about this skinny kid than those ravens we saw outside. *They* weren't supposed to die like that. You didn't cry for them. But you're practically hysterical over some human you don't even know. What's the matter with you?"

I scream into the dimness, ignoring my apprentice. *Where the hell is the veil?* I look over at the young man, and I see now that his cheeks are tearstained. He makes no motion as I approach him. He merely watches me with those lifeless eyes.

"Saving them isn't the job," my apprentice says. There's practically a growl in his voice. "God, are you always this sentimental? What's the big deal, anyway? Do you cry over every reap?" When I say nothing, he continues. "Jesus Christ, I've heard of ravens who fall in love with the marks, but this is out of control. Look at you! You're a wreck! And he's just some broken imbecile who couldn't even keep himself out of danger!"

Shut up, I think, anger burning in my chest. *Just shut up and let me think. There's no veil. That has to mean something. There has to be something we can do to save this kid.*

"Look, he shit himself. Look! Teacher, he's a goner. Man, what a loser. Where's the damn veil so we can kill this idiot and get on with our day?"

I want to bash my apprentice's face in. I want to claw his eyes out. I want to rip out his tongue.

But I don't do any of these things. I hop up onto the young man's stomach and settle down as gently as I can. I stare up into his eyes, and still, he doesn't move.

"You're seriously harshing my vibe, man," my apprentice snarls as he drags his feet through the blood, smearing it over the floor. "This was supposed to be *fun*. My first job! And you're acting like somebody pissed all over your nest! It's not that serious."

Finally, the light in the room shifts ever so slightly. I look up to see that the veil has finally descended, giving us a way out. I press myself away from the man and examine him for his cord. It's attached at the foot. I throw him once last glance. His jaw has gone slack, and his mouth hangs open.

The tag with my name on it unfurls.

"There it is!" Apprentice shouts. "Jesus Christ, finally! What do I do? Should I grab it? Do you want me to kill him?"

I feel dizzy. Do I want my apprentice to kill this man? I don't. I don't want anyone to kill him. He should be in college, or at his part-time job, or lying in bed with his sweetheart. He should be anywhere but here, dying naked and alone, covered in blood and shit. But Apprentice is right about one thing: saving him isn't the job. It never was.

"You take it," I say wearily. "You've earned it."

With a squeal, my apprentice sweeps in and catches the man's glittering cord in his claw. I see no physical change as his soul lifts free of his body. His eyes do not close; their light merely goes out.

"Take it up and out," I say. "Lead with your beak; that's how you cross the veil. Take it to the Near Shore. You know the way, don't you?"

Apprentice beats his wings, pure adrenaline raging through his body as he trembles with pleasure. "Of course I do," he says, "but aren't you coming with me?"

I shake my head. "Not this time," I say.

I watch as my apprentice shoots upward, his beak perfectly puncturing the veil, taking the young man over to the Other Side. I know I should go as well; it's part of the training. But I can't stand to be with him another minute. I need space.

I don't have much time to sit around feeling sorry for myself, as the veil is already thinning and will soon be gone. If I don't want to go out the way I came, I need to go through the veil, too. But before I do, I take one last look at the dead man slumped on the floor amid his own blood. I think of him and the wingless ravens rotting in cages outside.

And before I lose my head completely, I take flight, rising through the veil, taking the long way home.

CHAPTER FIVE

October 20th

I DIDN'T SLEEP IN MY NEST for days after that. I was too upset to be alone; I worried that I would have nightmares of my apprentice hopping around in the young man's blood. Instead, I crashed under overpasses, keeping company with the homeless. I scavenged sleeping quarters in attics with ring-tail cats. Anything to avoid sleeping alone.

Today, I'm having breakfast with Magpie, she feasting on a peach and I on a fried chicken wing. The thing I love most about Magpie is that she rarely asks me about myself. In another bird, I might write off this lack of curiosity as self-absorption. But in the magpie, it's as refreshing as a spring zephyr. She's the only companion in my world that doesn't remind me of death. It's easy to love someone like that.

"They're doing Shakespeare in the park," she says through a mouthful of sweet mush.

"Who?"

The magpie shrugs, fluffs her gleaming white feathers in my direction. "Oh, *I* don't know. They. I saw them last night setting up the stage. Would you like to go watch?"

I swallow my bite of chicken. "What, right now?"

Magpie nods. "Yes. Are you busy? You don't have another job, do you?"

I shake my head. "Thankfully, no." I tilt my head toward her. "Why, did you hear something?"

"Hear something? I wouldn't say that. More like…sensed."

I narrow my eyes at Magpie, who has the decency to lower her eyes demurely. "What do you *sense*?" I ask.

"I sense you had a bad day recently. You lost something valuable. I can see it all over you. We deal in treasure, you know. So I can tell."

I heave a sigh, take another bite of chicken. "It wasn't a good reap," I agree. "My apprentice…I think there might be something wrong with him. He was so cavalier about the whole thing. Didn't take any of it seriously. He was so *jazzed* to kill this person, and I—"

I stop speaking when I notice the way Magpie has turned her head slightly and chews more slowly. She doesn't want to hear the gruesome ins and outs of my work. I can't say I blame her. "I'm sorry. I got carried away."

"It's all right," she says. "But I do wonder."

"Wonder what?"

She takes a second before she says, "You say there might be something wrong with him because he was excited to do the job. But, Raven, isn't that how you were when you started? He's green; isn't that possibly all it is? Maybe he just needs proper training. Do you think?"

Grudgingly, I do see her point. And while I was never as irreverently gung-ho as my apprentice, I'm sure I toed the line. Maybe I've done my apprentice a disservice. Perhaps he deserves another chance.

"Heard and acknowledged," I say, nodding. "Thank you, Magpie. I'm glad I can count on you for good advice."

"I don't know about that," she says with a grin, "but at least you know where to come for a good meal." She pushes the last of her peach toward me with a sparkle in her eye, and I devour it gladly.

THE NEXT MORNING, I'm soaring over Bouldin Creek, one of the oldest neighborhoods in south Austin. In the middle of a busy east-west thoroughfare sits a small café with green-and-white striped awnings partially hidden from view by the giant oak tree that sits out front, overhanging the street. I circle the café a few times, hoping to see my benefactor outside smoking a cigarette. When I don't see her, I settle in the oak tree and begin to sing.

You can't call what I do singing if I'm honest. It's more of a discordant braying, an awful sound that causes passersby to throw painful looks in my direction. Sometimes they shout at me to shut up. But I'm not here for their entertainment; I'm trying to alert the proprietor of my presence. I'm launching into my third round of song when the front door opens, and an old woman tumbles out, hands on the hips I know give her trouble as she squints into the leaves.

"You shut up with all that noise!" she grumbles, reaching into her apron pocket. "You start scaring my customers away, I'll shoot you myself." She retrieves a sandwich from her pocket and tears it into pieces that she tosses out on the sidewalk.

Nearly as soon as the food hits the pavement, a plague of grackles invades. The old woman stomps her foot and shoos them with her hands, but the grackles aren't dissuaded. They merely dodge her attacks and flutter their wings as they dart toward the food that's meant for me.

I leap to the ground, landing in the middle of the grackle infestation. I spread my swings and screech at them, sending them skittering into the street, jibbering and jabbering as they go, throwing dirty looks over the wings. I pick up the pieces of sandwich my benefactor has provided and offer a kind chirp as thanks.

"Yeah, I like that," she says, a wicked smile on her face. "You show them who's boss. I hope you like tuna fish. Come back tomorrow, and I'll have pancakes."

I eye the old woman carefully, wondering whether she might be the answer to my dilemma. She can't have more than ten or so years left to live. She's got a generous heart—she feeds me every time I see her. I add her as a possible contender for Carrie's baby. I have ten days to make my final decision as I can't cart the soul away until Halloween night.

The last of the sandwich eaten, my belly full and hunger sated, I take off into the sky in search of another name to add to my list.

A few blocks away from the café is a small, tumbledown neighborhood in modest disrepair. The houses aren't well-tended, and it's evident from the height of the weedy lawns that there is no HOA. Still, it looks peaceful, and many of the houses have gotten into the holiday spirit—skeletons, witches, and a healthy crop of tombstones decorate the yards. Artificial spiderwebs climb the trees. Pumpkins rot on porches. This neighborhood feels like home, and so I circle above until I see movement through the leaves.

Coming slowly up one of the tree-lined streets is a small moving van. It pulls into the driveway of a white-and-blue shuttered house with a "For Rent" sign out front. The van rolls to a halt, and the door opens. A man who appears to be in his mid-thirties steps from the vehicle and runs a hand through his hair as he surveys his surroundings. His back is straight and his shoulders square. He's a bit too thin, but not unreasonably so. Dark hair frames a gentle face, a bit weathered around the eyes. He looks like the sort of person who listens to Chopin but also enjoys 80s action movies unironically. I like him already.

He pulls a set of keys from his pocket and heads to the front door. It takes him a few moments to get the keys in, but eventually, the door swings open. He looks in but doesn't step inside. Instead, he pushes the door as wide as it will go before heading back to the van and pulling up the back gate.

As he climbs inside, I fly a little lower, looking for a good place to perch when I see a young woman, probably in her mid-twenties, crossing the street toward the man's house. She's carrying two sweating cups of iced tea.

"You the new guy I heard about? From out of town?"

The man pops his head out from the moving truck, his expression a cross between dismay and surprise. But when he sees the woman and her easygoing smile, he returns it with only a smidge of self-consciousness. "Guilty," he says, hopping down to the ground. He wipes his palms on his jeans before extending a hand, then dropping it with a laugh. "I was gonna offer to shake, but it looks like you've got your hands full."

"Oh, right. Well, this one's for you," the woman says, pressing a cup into his hands. She nods toward the "For Rent" sign. "Walt's a friend of mine. He told me somebody new was moving in today. I thought I'd be neighborly." She looks a bit embarrassed at the admission, but the fellow doesn't seem to notice.

He accepts the cup and takes a big swig before saying, "Well, you didn't have to do that, but I do appreciate it. Walt's a great realtor. I probably looked for a house for six months on my own, but everything kept falling through. Rough market, Austin. But as soon as I found Walt, things just seemed to work out. How long've you known him?"

The woman shrugs offhandedly. "I don't know, maybe three, four years. I'm Leigh."

The man takes another deep gulp, then wipes his mouth with the back of his hand which he then extends. "Paul," he says. "Nice to meet you." They shake hands, and the tension between them fizzles a bit. I like this about humans. All it takes is a little bit of familiarity and ritual, and you earn each other's trust implicitly. "You live around here?"

She thrusts a thumb over her shoulder, indicating a squat, pink building with a dying lawn. "Yeah, that's me over there. Me and my roommate, Kit. You probably won't see a lot of her, though. She's a night owl. Plays in a band. They're pretty good, though. You into live music?"

Paul considers this a moment before chuckling and shaking his head. "I know it's lame, but not really. I guess I prefer to keep to myself and live performances kind of give me second-hand embarrassment. Does that make sense?"

The woman laughs then, a pretty sound like wind chimes. "Well, I mean, I understand the words coming out of your mouth. I'm just kidding, yeah, I get it. Still, in the interest of being neighborly, I might invite you out sometime."

I can't help but grin to myself, for here is another example of how bad you humans are at communication. This lovely young woman is offering courtship to this gangly, middle-aged hermit, but he doesn't notice. What's more, she doesn't notice that he doesn't notice. It's enough to drive a raven to an early grave. Figuratively speaking, of course.

Paul clears his throat and rubs the back of his neck. "So how long have you lived in the neighborhood?"

Leigh hrmms, cocks her head to the side as she thinks. "Little over three years, I think? It's a nice area. It kinda feels like the middle of nowhere, but it's just a quick bike ride across the bridge. You work downtown?"

Paul licks his lips, a slight pink blush rising into his cheeks. He breaks eye contact with the woman and fidgets a bit. "Ah, no. I'm sort of between jobs right now."

Abashed, Leigh waves this information away with a flick of her hand. "Oh, well, don't worry. The economy is booming here. You'll find something in no time. You work in tech?"

Again, the fellow searches for less awkward territory as he shifts his weight from foot to foot. "No, I'm worthless with computers. I used to be a teacher," he says. His eyes flicker to life then. "Sixth grade. But I've sort of been on sabbatical for a few years now." He flashes her a rueful smile. "I'm not sure what I want to do next, to be honest. I was thinking of going back to school and starting over, but I don't know. What do you do?"

Leigh is too quick to answer, the way some people are when they feel they've made a faux pas. "Nothing. I mean, I work at the gardening center." Her chagrined smile widens as she beckons toward her yard. "Not that you can tell by the state of my lawn."

Paul laughs and finishes off his iced tea, handing Leigh the empty cup. "I could help you with that. I know I probably don't look like it, but I've got a green thumb. When I was teaching, I always had a garden in my backyard. Some of my students would come over on the weekends and help me plant and harvest vegetables. I grew everything from tomatoes to okra to green beans. You'd be surprised what you can grow in just a few square feet of dirt." He rolls his eyes, his face growing pink again. "Well, maybe *you* wouldn't be surprised," he amends with an awkward chuckle. "Didn't mean to mansplain you."

Leigh grins and takes a sip of her iced tea. "Oh, I know what you mean. My mom grows award-winning roses, which is no small feat, let me tell you. She dedicates her whole life to it. My little sister still lives at home, and she has to help Mom with making the fertilizer. She fucking hates it."

Paul chuckles and groans, nodding as he rocks back onto his heels. "Award-winning roses. Wow, that's something. I imagine that can't be easy to do in Texas. It seems like the heat would be too much for them. Your mother must be amazing at what she does. You must be proud."

"You got that right," Leigh agrees, her posture straightening at the small praise. Her cheeks glow. "She's something else, my mom. She raised us alone, too. We were everything to her. Center of her universe. I don't have kids yet so I guess I can't understand, but she would have done anything for us.

Well, anything except give up her flowers. Everybody's got their weakness, I suppose. My mom's is her award-winning roses."

Paul nods and smiles graciously, but I can tell from the subtle clues in his stance and body language that he's not interested in Leigh's mother or award-winning roses. Still, he listens and smiles and nods and hrmms because he was raised right and knows how to feign a healthy interest. I feel a twist of something in my belly. I think it might be hope. "Hmm. Well, if you have to have a weakness, that's a good one, right? I mean, roses. That's worthwhile. You plant them, you feed them, prune them, protect them. And then you have a beautiful piece of living art that you've had a direct hand in shaping. I imagine that's very satisfying."

Leigh cocks her head to the side and squints, a playful smile on her face. "Is that why you became a teacher?"

Paul blushes and shrugs. His bashfulness is heartwarming. "Oh, I don't know. Maybe. Yeah, sure. It's something like that anyway. So you have a younger sister? How old?"

"Sixteen," Leigh says with a frown. "That's such a shit age. I wouldn't be a teenager again for all the money in the world."

Paul matches Leigh's frown, blows out his breath with puffed cheeks. "Yeah, I know what you mean. Sixteen is practically an adult, so you're in this tough place. Eleven, twelve is better. Old enough to have opinions but young enough to be molded. Also, less attitude."

A dog starts barking close by, and the noise is too much for the two strangers to talk over. The conversation lags. I'm drawn to Paul and his easygoing nature, the way he engages this young woman with such warmth and kindness even though he's immune to her feminine wiles. In my mind's eye, I can see him as a young boy, playing catch in the backyard or smearing jelly over white bread in the kitchen. Yes, he would make an enchanting son for Carrie.

But similarly, I am attracted to the young woman. Her

energy is youthful and bright and unsullied, and she might also be a perfect fit for Carrie's womb. I need to know just a little bit more first. I can't risk her having some god-awful secret, like nose-picking. Gross.

"Anyway, thanks for the iced tea," Paul says, gesturing toward the two empty cups Leigh now holds. "I've got a lot of unpacking to do, so. But I suppose I'll…"

A car pulls up, the windows rolled down. The driver sticks her head out and gives a low whistle. "Hey, hot stuff, what's a girl like you doing in a shit hole like this?"

Eyes wide, Leigh spins around and, seeing who it is, begins to laugh. She swats playfully at the woman in the car, then presses her hand to her chest. "You scared me, asshole! What are you doing here?"

"I was just in the neighborhood and thought I'd see what you were up to. About to grab some sushi. You hungry?"

Leigh glances to Paul who gives a small wave and mouths, "Nice to meet you" as he melts into the background toward the house. Leigh dashes to her own house, leaves her cups on the stoop, and hurries back across the road to slide into the front seat of her friend's car. Leigh leans out the window and waves to Paul who gives an amicable wave in reply. They pull away, and I watch for a moment, trying to decide whether or not I should follow. There's a delectable sushi place not far as the crow flies, but I can't imagine I'll have a decent vantage point from which to listen to their conversation. As lovely a creature as she was, then, it seems Leigh is off the hook. So I return my attention to Paul.

He's back in the truck, shuffling boxes around before hauling them one by one into the house. He doesn't have much, and I can't see any furniture. A perpetual bachelor? Or perhaps newly divorced? He did say he's been on sabbatical, so maybe he's just returned from one of those New Age retreats in Tibet or India or somewhere. I can't imagine why you people indulge in those things. You don't have to go to a foreign country for enlightenment. All you have to do is look around.

I watch Paul for a short while before he emerges once more and wipes his face with the hem of his shirt. He stands in the driveway, hands on his hips before heading to the sidewalk and taking a left.

Curious, I follow behind, finding a sweet perch in the neighbor's tree. Paul is moving slowly, shuffling his feet as he trudges up to his neighbor's front door. He pauses a moment at the door before giving the doorbell a decisive push. After a few moments, a woman answers. She doesn't open the screen as she asks, "Hi, can I help you?"

Paul's smile has evaporated, and suddenly he's all business, his expression cold and his eyes clouded. "Hello, ma'am. I just moved into the house next to yours. My name's Paul Andrews, and I'm required under the terms of my release to inform you that I'm a registered sex offender."

The woman's gasp is audible from my perch as she slams the door in Paul's face. He smirks and backs away, reaching into his pocket. A moment later, he's looking down at a photograph of a girl no older than eleven or twelve. He pauses to caress the photo with his fingertips before sliding it gently back into his pocket.

I utter a screeching croak as I drop down from my vantage point. Paul jumps in his skin as I career past him, close enough to catch a tangle of his hair in my talons. He squeals as I zip by, a clawful of his hair clutched in my grasp.

There's an old wives' tale about birds and human hair. They say that if a bird makes a nest from your locks, you'll feel it pecking at your head for the rest of your life or until you lose your mind. I take small comfort in this as I put distance between the molester and me. I know a family of woodpeckers that could use a nice addition to their nest.

I arrive home to find my apprentice sniffing about, poking through my things. I don't keep much. I'm not a packrat like the magpies, but I do have a few accouterments to make my perch more comfortable: a collection of particularly sweet sticks I've yet to integrate into my nest and a few gourmet nuts I've stolen from local squirrels. When my apprentice sees me, he jumps backward, smiling too broadly and pretending he has done nothing wrong.

I tuck the hair underneath the sticks and turn to my apprentice. "You're back," I say. "How did it go? Returning the soul, I mean."

"Man, it was *awesome*!" he nearly shouts. I grimace at his choice of words. "There was another reaper coming in as I arrived. I wasn't sure what I was supposed to do. By the way, that other reaper? He said you were supposed to accompany me home on my first reap." My apprentice gives me a dubious look, but I keep my face collected until he shakes it off and continues. "Anyway, I wasn't sure where I was supposed to go, but the other reaper showed me. I think he passed over okay. He didn't have as many friends and family waiting for him as I expected."

I raise my wing in a slight shrug. "Yeah, sometimes they don't have anyone. I'm not sure which is sadder; when they leave their loved ones behind, or when there's no one on the Other Side to greet them." Once again, a jolt of bitterness nips at my heart.

"So, question."

I lift a weary eyebrow. "Yeah?"

"Have you come up with a nickname for me yet? I heard some of the other reapers talking. They said you should have given me a name by now. So I wondered if you've given it any thought."

I haven't, but now that the question is put to me, I realize he's right. I lean on my intuition and blurt out the first appropriate response I can think of. "Grackle."

He's startled by that answer, and I take a grim pleasure in that. He was probably expecting something like Rocket or

Boss or Tiger or, ugh, Killer. But he takes it in stride, fluffing his feathers and stamping his feet in what I assume is a false show of pride.

"Grackle," he says, trying the name on for size. "All right, I guess. That'll take some getting used to."

I smile, then feel guilty for my causticity, then feel chuffed at my cleverness, then feel guilty once again as I think of Magpie's gentle admonition to be patient with my recruit. After all, it's not like I don't have sins in my past. I fret and sigh. I'm not sure how I'm supposed to feel.

"Anyway," Grackle is saying, oblivious to the gamut of emotions I have just run through in the space of several seconds, "the Virago says we have another mission today. She wants you to give me a tour of the city. She says I can't reap without knowing the city like—"

"Like the underside of your wing. I know," I say. "Did she give any particular indication of where we should begin?"

Grackle nods. "She says to head to Colorado Street. There's something she wants us to see."

I sigh at the festering rot of my luck. "Colorado Street? That's…pretty non-specific. Just that? No landmark or anything?"

Grackle shrugs. "That's all she said. I figured you'd know what she meant."

"I rarely know what the Virago's thinking," I admit. "Well, okay. If we have the length of an entire street to canvas, I guess we'd best get going."

We launch into the sky, Grackle smiling and full of unfettered enthusiasm. I am feeling notably less excited because I know the Virago hasn't merely sent us on a sightseeing mission.

Somewhere on Colorado Street, someone is about to die.

CHAPTER SIX

October 21st

RUSH-HOUR TRAFFIC BEGINS early in this part of town, and as we fly toward Colorado Street, I take inventory of the many different vehicles on the roads below. I can't help but think that in one of those SUVs or roadsters or minivans is a soul that would delight Carrie if only I could nab it from this world. But with Grackle at my side, all I can do is think about it. I can't fly into one of those windows or perch atop a hood ornament at a red light. The streets are clogged with souls that could be The One if only I had the time and privacy to investigate.

As we soar above downtown, I point out the various landmarks that the Virago will want my apprentice to know. "That's Congress Bridge," I say, indicating with the tip of my wing. "An enormous colony of bats lives there. Every night as sunset, you can see them migrating out from under the bridge. It looks like a galactic swarm of birds to the untrained eye. It's an astounding view. If you're good," I joke, "I'll take you to see it some evening."

I can practically feel Grackle rolling his eyes at my condescension. "Oh, won't you *please*," he breathes, pitching his voice high and coquettish. "I would *so* like to see a *bat*."

"Have it your way," I say. I bank slightly to the right, and Grackle follows suit. "That building over there is Jo's Coffee. A guy named Randy or Andy eats there on Thursdays, and he'll give you his pizza crust if you wait out the grackles. He hates them as much as I do, so he never—"

"You hate grackles?" Grackle asks.

I falter. "Hate is probably too strong a word." It's not. "But pretty much any raven around these parts would say he hates those frigging icterids," I say. "Do yourself a favor and keep your distance from them. They'll make you look bad and take your earnings while they're at it. Grackles are bad news."

"I'll remember that." His promise is so sober I feel bad for a moment at lending him the name. "If I run into any, I'll make sure to show those weak-ass bitches who's boss!"

The moment of my feeling bad has passed.

"Okay, up here on your left is Republic Square. I doubt you'll ever have to reap anyone there, at least not until summer. Some people do pass out from heatstroke from time to time. It's where they host these downtown farmer's markets."

This piques Grackle's interest. "You ever done that? Had to reap someone in broad daylight?"

"Sure. We all do it at one point or another. In Austin, it's not usually anything nefarious like a murder. Though, back in May, I had to reap a bride at her own wedding."

I hear a sharp intake of breath. "That's *so cool*," he breathes.

A shiver runs down my spine, and if I weren't mid-air, I would spin around and catch Grackle by the throat, forcing him to look me in the eye and say that again. I'd put the fear of God in him, make him realize what an outrageous thing he's just said. Instead, I merely growl at him. "Is it? It's *cool* to kill a woman on what's supposed to be the happiest day of her life?"

Grackle whistles. "Uh, yeah? I mean, it's pretty gruesome.

But it kinda makes you famous, right? Or like, *infamous.* Nobody who was there will ever forget that day."

His words strike a chord with me, but not in a good way. He is, of course, vocalizing exactly how I've come to feel about this profession. Nobody can unsee or forget the carnage I leave behind. It's not the legacy I want for myself.

Carrie, I think silently. *I didn't forget. I'm doing the best I can.*

"During the summer," I continue, "heat stroke, heart attack, and aneurysms are our biggest culprits. Other times of the year, it's car wrecks. Drunk drivers, mostly. You see a lot of them. We do get some stabbings, though violent deaths have been steadily decreasing over the past few years. The police want to take credit for that, but I think it has more to do with the flourishing economy. Do you know what Maslow's pyramid is?"

I only realize Grackle hasn't been listening when he calls out, "Hey, who's that up there?"

I follow Grackle's line of sight to see a mere dot perched on top of a stately white building up ahead. I can barely make out the shape, and I suck in my breath in surprise. How did he even *see* that from so far away? If he hadn't pointed it out, I might have missed it altogether.

Grackle and I begin our descent as we approach the fellow perched on the roof. From a distance, I had thought that perhaps he was a rook, but up close, now I see that he's a jackdaw. And, of course, this is Colorado Street.

My pulse quickens as an old nursery rhyme whispers through my mind. *Jackdaw, jackdaw stay away. Sit not on my roof to play. Jackdaw, jackdaw go and fly. No one here must needs to die.*

As we approach, the jackdaw glances up at us with a huge smile, hopping from foot to foot. He doesn't say anything as we land, and, after a moment, returns his attention to some distant point, the subject of which I cannot discern. I scuttle over to him, putting my best foot forward. "How's it going?"

The jackdaw nods good-naturedly. "Oh, splendid, fine. And yourself?"

"Well, you've just made it better," I admit. "I thought we were gonna have to fly around all damn day. We're on a tour of the area," I explain. "Wouldn't have known to stop here if it weren't for you."

The jackdaw makes understanding noises. "This is a business trip for the two of you, then," he says.

"A business trip to the Governor's Mansion," I say. "And since you're here, and we're here, that can only mean one thing."

The jackdaw nods. "Quite right. And I don't mind saying, I'm delighted to see you as well, though for opposing purposes, I daresay. On the one wing, I have a question I'd very much like to ask you."

As I'm in no particular hurry to tend to my next reap, I nod, inviting him to ask. "All right, what is it?"

The fellow grins. "It's actually…more of a *riddle* than a question."

"Oh, no," I groan, a low rumble in my throat. "Listen here, Jackdaw, if you're about to ask—"

"Why is a raven like a writing desk?"

I pounce on him then, tackling him to the roof. The jackdaw, being much smaller than me, squirms underneath my weight, but still he's laughing as he shouts out, "P-Poe wrote on both!"

I peck him a few times right in the ribs, enough to sting but not enough to hurt him. He's still laughing as he rolls onto his side beneath my claws, shouting to Grackle. "Better watch out for this one!" he chirps. "He's stark *raven* mad!"

I attack him again, this time going for the underside of his wing, and his laughter turns into shrieking. I must have hit a ticklish spot. He staggers to his feet, the laughter still dribbling from his beak. "Heard that one, have you? Oh, I love that joke," he says, rubbing the spot where I've nipped him. "I can't resist using it any time I run into you lot."

I roll my eyes and make a get-on-with-it motion with my wing. "All right, you've had your fun. Spill it, Jackdaw. The joke was on the one wing. And on the other?"

Jackdaw smears the last tears of laughter from his eyes and straightens himself out. "Oh, right. Well, on the one wing, I wanted to shame you with my favorite joke, but on the *other* wing, I'm relieved to see you here. You see, I've been sitting here for the better part of the afternoon waiting to catch a glimpse of the royal family, but I haven't seen anyone come in or out of the building all day. And no guards, either. How do they keep themselves safe? Do they have some magical protection we don't have at home?"

"You must be from London!" I exclaim. When the fellow pirouettes and twitters, I know I've guessed right. "I thought I recognized your accent. *You're* a long way from home. You know, if you wanted to get a look at the royal family, you'd be better off sitting on the other side of the street. You can't see jack-shit from on top of the building."

"I know," the jackdaw sighs, "and that's why I'm glad you've finally arrived. Fate compelled me to sit here. But now that you've found me, it means I can leave." He cocks his head at me. "It's true, right? If you hadn't seen me, you'd have kept on flying?"

I nod. "Probably. We might have kept flying for hours."

The jackdaw looks satisfied with this answer as he turns to face my apprentice. "What about you? You interested in seeing the royal family?"

Grackle lifts an eyebrow and clears his throat. "Well, first of all, they're not royal. The governor is an elected official, and his family is nothing special at all. And as for guards, they do have them, just not the way you're used to. They don't stand around outside the Mansion wearing ridiculous hats like those guys at Buckingham," he says.

The jackdaw hrmms and makes a face that reads *thanks-for-the-info-you-giant-horse's-ass*, but Grackle doesn't even notice. "Well, anyway, my mentor's right. If I wanted to see the *governor* and his family, I'd be better off perching across the street."

"You would have a better view," the jackdaw says. "But you'd be failing at your job."

Grackle side-eyes him, clearly unimpressed with the English jackdaw's scoping out of the non-royal family from a disadvantaged location. "How's that?"

I take the opportunity to do a bit of mentoring and indicate the jackdaw with a flutter of my wing. "Jackdaws are corvids, which means he's our cousin. Which means when it comes to our line of work, jackdaws are our allies. Does he look stupid to you?"

Grackle makes a face like he wants to say yes. "No?"

"Right. Jackdaws are not stupid. So if he's sitting here in a terrible location for sightseeing, don't you think you should question *why that is?*"

Now Grackle sighs and rolls his eyes. "*Fine.* What's so special about a jackdaw on top of the Governor's Mansion?"

Now, it's my turn to preen. I puff out my chest and say, with as much prestige as I can dredge up, "A jackdaw on a rooftop means a new arrival. And for us, what is a new arrival?"

Grackle's eyes go wide as he finally takes my meaning. "New arrivals are the souls of the dead that we bring to the Near Shore," he breathes.

I nod. "Exactly. You see a jackdaw on top of a building, you should investigate. It means someone inside is knocking on death's door."

Grackle squeals and his beak drops open in astonishment, looking from me, to the jackdaw, and back again. "I've never heard that before," he breathes. "Is it true? Is he pulling my leg?" He directs this question to the British tourist.

"Afraid he's right," he says. "But I can't tell you *who* will perish."

My apprentice frowns. "Because you don't know?"

The jackdaw lifts an eyebrow. "Because it's a secret."

Grackle leans in and stamps his feet. "A secret? And you can't be persuaded to tell?"

The British fellow makes a nasty face and is about to retort when I interrupt. "Don't mind him; he's new. Doesn't understand what he's just said. Has no idea at all about your business," I say.

The jackdaw fluffs his feathers and sniffs. "Well, I suppose there's no harm in plain ignorance," he says, still glaring at my charge, "but you'd better fill him in. Big mouth like his is bound to get you into trouble, you go around insulting the wrong people."

"Jackdaws deal in secrets," I say. "If you tell a jackdaw a secret, he'll die with it laced in his tail feathers; he'll never tell another soul. And if you want information *from* a jackdaw—information he's earned of his own accord, of course, not that which has been entrusted to him—he'll make you a trade. One secret for one piece of information. Tit for tat."

I glance at the jackdaw to see if my explanation meets his approval, and as he returns his gaze to the city, it seems it has. "Speaking of information, Jackdaw," I say, "you haven't spied a way into the house, have you?"

The jackdaw shakes his head. "Nope. Like I said, no one has come in, and no one has gone out. Place is locked up tight. Can't imagine what must be happening inside. Trade secrets, maybe? Perhaps confidential conspiracies?"

I shake my head. "Probably nothing as exciting as that. Just someone dying; that's my guess. Question is: who?"

The jackdaw scrunches the feathers around his beak. "I imagine that answer will reveal itself in short order. However…"

The look on his face tells me that he knows something, and

since I don't have the first idea how to get inside the Mansion to complete my mission, I take a step forward, lowering my ear toward the jackdaw's beak. "You have something you want to say?"

The jackdaw makes a face. "I might know *something*," he says, "if you have a secret to trade."

I look to Grackle, who has been studying our exchange with a journeyman's intensity. "Well?" I ask him. "This is *your* training. Should be your secret on offer. What've you got?"

My apprentice looks troubled as he shakes his feathers and stamps his feet. "A secret? Me? I don't have any secrets," he lies.

"You lie," Jackdaw says. "Everyone has secrets. And those who claim *not* to have secrets usually have the best secrets of all."

"Well, not me," Grackle says, cutting his eyes at both of us as though daring us to try him again. "Why are you picking on the recruit, anyway? You say it's my training, but *you're* the teacher. Why don't *you* cough something up?"

Both pairs of eyes turn to me, expectant. I open my beak to retort, then close it again. I do have a secret. Of course I do. And the jackdaw, who is no fool, will see me for a charlatan if I pretend to have nothing. And anyway, one of us has to give something up: I need all the help the jackdaw can give.

"I suppose I do have something I can share. But it's for the jackdaw's ears only," I say, giving my apprentice a sharp look. "You step over that way and don't even look over here."

Grackle looks wounded as he takes several small hops backward. "Have it your way," he says.

I clear my throat and move in closer to the jackdaw, who is eyeing me with curiosity. "It must be good what you have," he says, his voice low. "Most birds aren't so keen to make a big deal of it."

"It's not that," I say, although it is. "He's a recruit. I have to make him fear me, so he obeys without question. Questioning me on the job can put both of us in danger."

"Even so," the jackdaw says, "I can tell you've got something good. So what is it, cousin? What's the secret you wish to exchange for entrance into the Mansion?"

I squeeze my eyes shut and lean forward, letting the words spill quickly from my beak before I can reconsider. When my plan for Carrie is revealed, the jackdaw flutters his wings in excitement, making sounds of sincere appreciation in his throat. "Now *that's* a good secret, mate. Best I've heard in a while."

I heave out a sigh and motion for Grackle to return. My apprentice does so, but begrudgingly, his pride still wounded. "All right, Jackdaw," I say. "What have you got? How do we get inside?"

The jackdaw jerks his head southward. "First-floor kitchen window's just that way. When I first got here, I saw a girl glancing out the window several times, like she was looking for something. Her name is Mary," he says. The look in his eyes indicates this is a meaningful piece of information, but I don't know what to make of it. "*Mary*," he says again.

I take a moment too long to process this, and before I can formulate a proper follow-up question, the jackdaw is already announcing his departure. "Well, chaps, I've been here long enough," he says. "I'm headed out to the Congress Bridge. Have you seen the bats?" he says to Grackle.

My apprentice shakes his head. "Not yet. But I'm sure we'll make it there soon. Teacher was telling me all about it. I hear it's badass."

"I do hope so," Jackdaw agrees. "I didn't come all this way to sit on top of a government building all day, that much is certain. At any rate, good luck to both of you. I hope you find what you're looking for."

"Wait! —"

But the jackdaw has already taken to the sky, soaring confidently in the wrong direction if he means to go to the Congress Bridge.

I grouse under my breath and curse. I've never known jackdaws to be swindlers, but I feel like I've grossly overpaid for the information I received. All he's given me is a name! What good is that supposed to be? What am I supposed to do with it? How is a name worth the price of my most closely-guarded secret?

I don't have time to be angry, however. Grackle is pacing up and down, the crease between his eyes deepening as he works the puzzle through his mind. "He said her name is Mary," my apprentice says ostensibly to me, but his voice is so low he could be thinking aloud. "Mary. What can it mean? How will it help us get inside the house?"

"Your guess is as good as mine," I grumble. "I was expecting him to divulge a secret underground passage that starts at the local taco joint or, barring that, the 4-1-1 on a drug dealer or a prostitute who sometimes comes over, but—"

An idea comes to me, stopping me mid-sentence. Could it be that simple?

There's only one way to find out.

"He said the young woman kept looking out the window," I say. "Like she was expecting something. Or, perhaps, someone."

Grackle frowns. "Yeah? So? Does that mean you have an idea? Do I get to kill someone now?"

"Hold your horses," I say, "and try not to be so goth. Here's what I'm thinking. How good are your vocal cords?"

Grackle clears his throat and stretches his neck. He begins to trill—a terrible sound that makes my skin crawl. I swat him in the face with the tip of my wing, pointed feathers catching him in the eyes, making him blink. "Knock that off!" I say. "Do you kiss your mother with that mouth?"

Grackle's confounded gaze back at me tells me he doesn't know this expression, and I sigh again. He hasn't been around enough humans to have picked up their colloquialisms, let alone their vocalizations—which means the task of getting into the house is going to fall to me.

"Listen up," I say. "If you're gonna be in the reaping business, you need to master a few things. One, you have to become adept at finding obscure ways into buildings. Two, you need to learn to find the nearly deceased quickly. Look for magpies or jackdaws, like you did today. That was good. I might've missed him, myself." At this small praise, Grackle's chest puffs up, and once again, I feel mildly like an ass for how I've treated him. "Three, you gotta know this city like the underside of your wing. And four, you need to get good at deception."

My apprentice nods vigorously, rubbing his wings together in anticipation. "Deception. Yeah, okay, I can do that." He pauses and throws me an innocent look. "Like what kind of deception?"

"Listen up." I take a deep breath and call out, in my best human voice, "Thank you! Please come again! Thank you! Please come again!"

My apprentice gasps in wonder and claps his wings. The look of astonishment on his face is rivaled only by his appreciation. "Wow, that was *awesome*! You sounded just like them! Where did you learn to talk like that?" he asks.

"I taught myself. It takes a lot of practice, and I can't say anything complicated. Mostly I can only repeat phrases I've heard over and over. But if you're going to get into places that humans don't want you in, it will behoove you to learn to imitate them. And I *think* that's what the jackdaw was trying to tell us today. We need to use Mary to get in, and I think I know how. Follow me."

We fly to the garden behind the Governor's Mansion, and I hop up to the sill to look inside the window. It's hard to tell with the glare, but I think I see a young woman inside. "Okay," I say. "Here's the plan. I'm going to scream to get the young woman's attention. With any luck, she'll hear me and run outside to see what all the commotion is about. As soon as that door opens, we need to dart inside, so you need to be ready to fly as fast as you can. Think you can do that?"

My apprentice bobs his head in excited confirmation. "Hell yeah, Teacher. You can count on me. Just tell me exactly what I need to do."

I frown. "I just did."

Grackle huffs. "You told me how we're getting inside. What do I do when we're *in* there?"

"Once we're inside, follow me. We have to be quick. I don't know when the veil will descend, so I don't know when we'll be able to shift skin. We have to be prepared to wear this skin right up to the death bed, though hopefully, it won't come to that. Do you understand?"

Grackle nods. "I'm ready. I was born for this."

I point to a nearby tree and Grackle flies up into it, settling down quietly. He quivers with so much excitement that the whole branch shakes. I open my beak as wide as I can and begin to scream.

"Mary! Mary!"

At first, nothing happens. I glance at Grackle, who is looking down at me with expectation. A beat goes by. Two. *Three*. And just as I'm about to begin my screaming one more time, the back door swings open and a young woman comes running outside. Her skin is blanched, eyes wide and round as the moon. Thankfully, she leaves the door ajar behind her. I scream one more time, attempting to throw my voice to conceal my location. "Mary!"

The young woman looks frankly terrified as she darts to the farthest corner of the yard. "Billy? Is that you? Where are you?"

I indicate for Grackle to follow me and, to his credit, he descends silently from the tree, and we both glide to the back door. We slip inside easily, our black feathers melding into the shadows. We follow along the far wall until the room splits into two halves: upstairs and downstairs. Instinct and familiarity with antebellum architecture lead me to believe the sickroom is upstairs, and it's there we will find our nearly deceased.

We fly up to the second floor, keeping out of the puddles of sunlight that pool along the Persian rugs. The doors on this level are mostly open, and we peek inside each room as we pass. Most of them are empty. None of them contain our mark.

I'm about to suggest that we check for a third floor when Grackle indicates a corridor that I hadn't noticed the first time. It's small and dark and leads away from the central part of the house. He cocks his head toward it. "I feel like what we're looking for might be down that way."

It feels strange to trust another bird's intuition, especially someone as green and untested as Grackle. But the Virago has delivered him to me, so he must have some innate—if latent— value as a reaper. Perhaps his instincts are better than my own; I don't know. And so I follow Grackle down the slender hallway.

We decide not to fly, instead taking small hops down the corridor. At the end of the hall is a closed door, and I hear soft murmuring on the other side. We press our heads against the wood, listening.

We hear the voices of children.

"When they come, will we see them, mama?"

A brief silence follows the question. Then another voice says, "When *who* comes, baby?"

"The angels," the little voice says. "When the angels come to take Grandma? Will we see them?"

Grackle looks at me and grins. "Not if I can help it," he says.

He slips into his death skin.

Somehow, I hadn't noticed the veil that has descended, allowing us to transition. Grackle has made the change elegantly and silently, and I follow suit. I feel my nerves flatten, and my heart rate settles down. Invisible within the veil, we are safe.

I lean towards Grackle and say, my voice low, "I think if we scratch at the door a little bit someone will come and investigate. That should be enough to get us inside."

Grackle gives a somber nod as I lift my foot and place my talons lightly against the wooden door. I give it a couple of small scratches, just enough to earn the attention of the inhabitants on the other side. Sure enough, after a few moments, a woman pokes her head out. She doesn't see anyone, so she opens the door a little bit wider, leaning out to look down the hall. That's when Grackle and I slip in, stepping into the darkness on the other side.

The room is dimly lit and smells like old people. In the center of the small room, an ancient woman lies against white sheets, her eyes closed. She looks like she's asleep. But it doesn't take a reaper to know she's the one marked for death today. The stink of it is all around her. I look for her glittering cord. The cord is there, attached by her ear, but my name is not. "Watch for the tag," I say. "We can't make a move until we see the tag."

We keep to ourselves, ensconced in a corner as the family continues to whisper and pray over the dying woman. The man, who I recognize now as the governor, lifts the old woman's hand in his own, caressing the thin, graying skin and biting down on his lips. I see a fair family resemblance between them if you discount that one is virile and young, the other just shy of a corpse. This woman is probably his mother.

"I love you so much," the man is saying, his voice breaking on his words. "But you can feel free to go now, Mama. You're moving on to a better place. The good Lord is waiting for you on the other side."

I see Grackle opening his mouth to object that no good Lord *is* waiting on the other side, but I throw him such a harsh look that he clamps his beak shut. Now isn't the time for casual jokes, even if our words are inaudible beneath the veil. The silence grows between them, the children beginning to whimper and cry. The mother tries to hush them, brushing their hair back from their foreheads and giving little kisses on their crowns. But it's plain that they know her death is coming. Grief lies thick in the room.

Suddenly, the woman's silver cord begins to sparkle, and the tag we've been waiting for unfurls itself. The tag, of course, has my name on it. At the same time that the tag appears, a younger woman has begun to speak. "Mama, everything I—"

No sooner has she started speaking than Grackle hurls himself towards the old woman's head with gusto. His veil-hidden wings beat against her face as he catches the cord in his talons and gives a triumphant yank. Her soul fairly pops from the body. The effect is ghastly. "I've got it!" he shouts. "Let's get the hell out of here. It stinks."

Shock. Horror. Disgust. Utter disbelief. These emotions take turns washing over me as I stare mutely at my apprentice, appalled at this irreverent behavior. The old woman doesn't die gracefully with a shuddering breath; she simply expires. Mid-breath, she was there one second, and then she wasn't.

The family cries out, the young woman covering her tearstained face with trembling hands. "No," she whispers. "Not yet. I wasn't ready. I didn't get to say goodbye."

Infuriated, I pierce through the veil with Grackle right behind. The incarnate world slips away as we rocket higher and higher toward the soft shores of the Other Side. I hear Grackle calling for me, but I ignore him, my blood boiling in my veins. It isn't until the Great Beyond shimmers into view that I turn toward Grackle, still trembling with fury as I scream, "What did you do? Why did you do that? I didn't tell you to do that!"

Grackle's expression is mystified. "What do you mean? The tag appeared! It had your name on it!"

"Yes," I spit, "but they weren't ready! You don't have to

take the cord the moment it appears! You can give them time to say goodbye! You didn't have to snatch their final moment away from them! It would have cost us nothing to let those people have a few more minutes alone with their loved one!"

Grackle's confusion morphs into exasperation. "I don't understand why you're so upset. It isn't our job to let them have their final words. If they had messages of love and affection for her, they should have told her while she was alive and able to profit from hearing them. Why should I care if a family has been too busy or selfish to make their love shown in their waking days? When it's time, I should be allowed to piss on the soul if like!"

Grackle's words are hot with a self-righteousness that makes my talons curl and my blood run cold. How can I explain to him that though humans are imperfect, they are still worthy of respect? How can I convey the depth of his defilement when he only sees reaping as a job?

"Apprentice," I say, making every effort to keep my tone calm, "death is a time of transition. It's dirty and scary, and it's the biggest event in a person's life. We have an honor-bound duty to make that transition as peaceful as possible for everyone — for the deceased and the family left behind."

But Grackle only rolls his eyes. "So *you* say. The Virago never said anything to me about making death peaceful. That's an idea *you* made up. *You're* the one with hang-ups about death. Why do you love them so much? For me, it's *fun*. I *like* killing them. Is that so wrong? It's what we signed up for! We're not priests; we're garbage collectors! Our job is to take out the trash. The sooner you realize that, the better off we'll both be!"

"Is that really how you feel about it?" I ask, horrified.

"Obviously," he says, "because that's the way it *is*."

I want to say something more, something profound, but I'm so disgusted with Grackle that I can't even look at him a moment longer. I turn my back and head back down to Earth alone. He's done this part of the job without me once; certainly, he can do it again. Protocol be damned. If the Virago wanted me to teach, she shouldn't have partnered me with that incorrigible brat. That stallion wants breaking, but I'm not the bird to do it.

I'll send word via Magpie in the morning. I'm done with Grackle. He can't be taught, at least, not by me. I don't have the stomach for it, so screw it, I'm out.

Today was supposed to be lovely. It was supposed to be a step closer to finding a soul for Carrie. It was supposed to be full of miracles and opportunity and hope.

Instead, I am filled with mourning and regret as I soar back down to Earth, leaving Grackle to laugh at me turning tail as he toys absently with the woman's soul clamped in his grubby claws.

CHAPTER SEVEN

October 25th

O F COURSE, THE VIRAGO tried to win me back.

She sent me all kinds of apologetic gifts. Magpie offered a poppet filled with mint and lavender that she'd found near a local organic linens store. The old woman from my favorite café showered me with chocolate chip cookies and peanut butter and jelly sandwiches—my favorite. The Virago has even tried sending crows to tell me my future, but I wouldn't entertain any of these things.

"Tell the Virago in no uncertain terms that I *will not* see Grackle again," I told the magpie as I refused her second attempt at gift-giving. This time she offered me a fluorescent pink shoelace shot through with metallic thread. (*"It would look so lovely snaked through the twigs of your nest!"* she'd countered wanly, undoubtedly thinking that if I didn't want it, she could put it to use herself.) "He's not fit to be a reaper, or at any rate, he's not fit to be my apprentice. I take the work very seriously. He treats death like a circus act. I can't stomach him. Find someone else."

The magpie fretted. "Raven, even if you don't want to see…Grackle, is it? What a funny nickname…you still need to return to work. People are suffering in their final moments. You need to bring a reprieve."

I offered an ill-tempered chortle. "Why doesn't she send Grackle to offer these poor people a reprieve? I'm taking a break. Indefinitely," I said, a finality in my voice that even Magpie wouldn't parry. "Now, please, leave me alone."

Magpie left me alone. And so did the Virago. I heard no more from either of them.

In the days that followed, I was too depressed even to pull myself from my nest. I sulked and slept, though I was plagued by bad dreams. On the fourth day, which is today, the only thing that rouses me from my torpor is the realization that my time for finding a soul for Carrie is drawing to a close; Halloween is a mere six days away. If I'm going to bring Carrie a blessing, I need to get over myself and recommit.

I shake myself free of my gloom and head out.

Rainbow Café is an outdoor coffee shop in the middle of a busy north-south thoroughfare. As usual, the café is over-flowing with Austinites busily typing on their laptops and chatting on their cell phones. As far as food goes, I usually have no luck here. The only snacks on offer are vegan treats in plastic wrappers, and the patrons rarely leave anything behind worth taking. But for people-watching, the location can't be beat.

It's late morning, and the crowd is a motley assembly of yoga babes, hippie chicks, brogrammers, venture capitalist assholes, and a smattering of students. As I scan the crowd looking for someone special—perhaps someone with an accent or lousy fashion sense or vitiligo—a couple of young women catch my attention. They're huddled together under a canvas umbrella and smell of Nag Champa and vetiver. Intrigued, I drop down and perch on a chair nearby.

"Have you talked to Tatum lately?"

The dark-haired woman shakes her head, sipping her coffee. "Nope. Have you?"

The other woman, whose hair is blue, shakes her head as well. "I was thinking of going by her place today. She hasn't snapped or tweeted anything since Sunday. She was really shaken up after the ritual last week. I want to see how she's doing."

The dark-haired woman fairly chokes on her coffee. Eyes round as the saucers on their table, she holds back a laugh. "What? So…you didn't hear? God, I thought the whole coven had heard about this. Maybe the entire fucking *town*."

Blue hair cocks her head to the side. "Heard what? What's going on?"

The other woman chuckles, shaking her head. She motions for her friend to lean in, lowering her voice. "She says she's been waking up next to dead guys," she whispers. "Hannah, get this. Apparently, and I heard this from Raven, Tatum claims that *twice* since Sunday night she's had sex with random guys she met on 6th Street, and then when she wakes up, they're dead."

Curious, I hop a bit closer. I haven't actually happened upon as many pagans as you might think, though they are abundant in Austin, or so I've heard. Nevertheless, an inordinate number of them have been named Raven. I guess I should be flattered? I'm not.

Hannah blinks, her face white. Her friend doesn't notice. "What?"

The other woman shakes her head. "I know, that was more or less my reaction, but Raven swears to Goddess that's what Tatum told her. I mean, I know Tatum's been through some stuff lately but coming up with this? It's ridiculous." She sits back in her chair, sighing. "I've known Tatum a long time, but this is a whole new level of bullshit. She's turning into a goddamned attention whore. What, we have a ritual—which, okay, really did not go as planned and was intense for everyone

—but as a result, she turns *straight*, starts fucking guys, and they wind up dead in her bed, and she has no idea how? Seriously? *Seriously?* I mean, what the hell? If she's not making it up, which is a big fucking *if*, somebody needs to call the cops, you know? Plus, I haven't read anything about missing or dead dudes in the Statesman. She needs to see a shrink. For real."

"Keep your voice down, Violet," says Hannah, looking around at the other patrons. Her brow is furrowed and her lips pursed. She sips her coffee, slinking down in her chair. "She really had sex with men?"

Violet guffaws. "Are you kidding? That's what you find most alarming about what I just told you?"

Hannah doesn't appear to be listening, however. Her eyes have misted over and gone to that far-away place usually reserved for dreamtime and grief. When she comes back, her eyes are cautious, her tone careful. "What does Raven think?"

Violet tosses her hair, makes a face. "Who cares what Raven thinks?"

Hannah frowns, a red flush creeping into her cheeks. "I do, that's why I asked. What does she think?"

"All right, damn, don't get all crazy on me. She thinks we need to sit down as a coven and discuss Tatum's behavior and see if we can come to an 'agreement' about what needs to happen next."

Hannah looks thoughtful as she chews on a piece of her bright blue hair. Then, "So, Raven doesn't believe her."

Violet laughs. "No, of course Raven doesn't believe her. Do you?"

Hannah shrugs, and though it is written all over her body, Violet misses the hesitation and distress. "I'm *worried* about her," Hannah says carefully. "I think Raven's right that we need to talk to her, but..." She shrugs, unable to finish the thought. "I don't think she's making it up. I mean, no, I don't believe...I mean, I think *something* is going on."

Violet waves off her friend's concerns, rolling her eyes.

"You like to see the good in people, Hannah," she explains. "And that's admirable and everything. But, and I say this for your own good, you need to get a fucking clue. Tatum is either full of shit or a psycho, and either way, she's not healthy for the group. She's got to go."

Hannah gives a non-committal *hrmm* before glancing down at her cell phone. "Shit, I gotta go," she says. "I'm late for an appointment. Will I see you tomorrow?"

Violet shrugs, waves her hand dismissively. "I don't know. I might skip this meeting. I'm kind of over everyone's bullshit, you know what I'm saying? I'll probably go to Krav Maga or something instead."

Hannah does not wait for more information. As she stands to leave, I don't know whether to stay behind and watch Violet or follow Hannah. Spiritual people have such interesting souls, and either woman could be a potentially brilliant daughter for Carrie. After quick consideration, I choose Hannah. There's something about her that make me curious to learn more about the secret she's keeping.

Or maybe I'm just a sucker for a chick with blue hair.

She gets into her car, and I follow her for a long while. She drives through the meandering streets of hill country before finally pulling up to a large, rambling home with a gazebo in the backyard. I don't know this part of town well and am not familiar with the kind of people who live here. And by that, I mean rich people. They don't seem to die as often as poor folks.

I wait for Hannah to ring the doorbell, my heart in my throat. If she goes inside, I won't be able to follow her, and then this whole expedition will have been a waste. The Virago, of course, can't help me with this mission: it isn't exactly on the agenda, not that the Virago and I are on the best terms right now, anyway.

No one answers the door, and after a while, Hannah moves to the side of the house and peers over the gate. Catching sight of someone, she waves. "Scarlet! Hey! Can I come in?"

Lounging under the gazebo is a woman, long, dark hair cascading over her shoulders. She's reading a book, which, upon hearing Hannah's voice, she sets down beside her. "Hannah? That you?"

Hannah presses her hand to the gate, pushing it open. She's smiling as she steps through, but it's false. Forced. "I know I shouldn't be here," she says. "But I really need to talk to you."

"It's fine," Scarlet says, looking around quickly before motioning for Hannah to sit beside her. "Noah's not here. Anyway, Mom always said you and I should spend more time together."

Hannah makes a face. "Yeah, so about that." Hannah sighs as she slips into place beside her sister, her expression once again growing dark. "Before she died, Mom was always telling me to try new things. To get out of my shell. Remember how she dragged me to her painting-with-wine class and then forced me into rock climbing?"

Scarlet smiles, nodding. "She only let you quit when you broke your wrist, and even then, she said you did it on purpose."

Hannah rolls her eyes. "Yeah, exactly. Well, she was right. Not about the painting and rock climbing but about trying new things. So I joined a coven six months ago."

It's Scarlet's turn to make a face, and she makes a patting motion with her hands. "Keep your voice down," she says. "You know I don't care about the kooky shit you're into, but if Noah hears, you'll freak him out. He wants us to raise Juniper as a Christian."

Hannah frowns. "I thought you said he wasn't here."

Scarlet shrugs. "He's not, but he could come home at any minute. I don't want him to, you know." She frowns and worries over her wedding ring with her thumb. "Catch us."

Hannah rolls her eyes but lowers her voice. "Anyway. Something crazy is going on, and you're the only person I can tell. At first, I thought it was just me, and I was willing to pass it off as...you know, grief shit from Mom dying or whatever. But it's something else."

Scarlet nods. "Go on."

Licking her lips and taking a deep breath, Hannah begins. "We had a ritual the other night. It was a pre-Halloween thing. We've been exploring aspects of the dark goddess, and we decided this was the right time of year to start working with her. So we did this ritual where we called on Lilith. Or Ardat Lili. Depends who you ask. Do you know who that is?"

Scarlet shakes her head. "Uh uh."

"In Jewish mythology, she was Adam's first wife. According to legend, she was kind of a Dom, and she didn't want to have missionary sex with Adam. She only wanted to have sex in the female dominant position."

Scarlet groans, rolling her eyes. "Oh my god, only you would join a religion that makes the Old Testament into some weird porno."

"Anyway," Hannah continues, ignoring the interruption, "Adam wasn't into it, so he gets rid of Lilith and trades her in for Eve. So Lilith gets pissed off and decides to destroy the patriarchy. So, in some circles, she's seen as this really powerful symbol of female empowerment."

Hannah doesn't notice as Scarlet's eyes flit nervously to the street, to the house, and back again. She shifts in her seat like she can't quite get comfortable.

"So that's the backstory. We do the ritual, and we invoke Lilith. And things didn't go well—a girl's robe caught on fire, this other girl fainted, shit like that. When it was over, I felt more lightheaded than usual. I talked with a few people, ate some soup and said my name aloud a few times but nothing helped. I couldn't ground; I felt like I was outside my body, watching my life instead of living it. You know, kind of how you feel after you've taken muscle relaxers with a beer."

Scarlet's face draws into a frown. "You're not supposed to do that," she scolds.

"Yeah, I know. So I was feeling weird all through the night, and I woke up feeling hungover and sick, even though I hadn't been drinking the night before."

At this, Scarlet's eyes narrow. "Hannah." She takes her sister's hand in her own. "Are you sure you weren't drinking? You can tell me. I won't judge you. But you can't—"

"I'm *sure*. I've been sober since I joined the coven." When her sister only nods, Hannah continues. "The next few days are a blur. I worked. I slept badly. I was having bad dreams that I couldn't remember. I was nauseated and tired all the time. Kind of like after Mom died." Scarlet nods, looks down into her lap.

Hannah tosses her hair back, blinks her eyes rapidly. "Five nights after the ritual, two nights ago, I couldn't sleep. I went to a hookah bar. Some guy with nice eyes sat down with me; we smoked for a while. The smoke made me sick. He offered to take me home. I asked him to take me to his place. We had sex."

Scarlet inhales sharply then, and Hannah looks away. I see now how different the sisters are—one, a recovering alcoholic who has turned to alternative religion and risky behavior to mourn the loss of her mother, the other working desperately to uphold a good-girl image to win the love and respect of an overly controlling husband. I think the goody-good sister would make a great daughter. I mentally add her to my list.

"I remember what I dreamed that night. There were these pools of blood and lava and pillars of fire leaping from the ground. These blackened corpses were screaming and trying to grab me. I was surrounded on all sides by fire and blood. I was in Hell, Scarlet. I'm sure of it."

Scarlet snorts, rolls her eyes. "People always talk about Hell like it's some underground volcano, but that's not what Hell is. Real Hell—" She stops suddenly, presses her lips together. Her eyes dart around the yard, searching. She closes her eyes and breathes in deeply through her nose. "Don't listen to me," she says. "Go on. Sorry for interrupting."

Hannah frowns. "So, I guess old habits die hard because I started reciting the Lord's prayer. But you know how sometimes in dreams your words are like molasses? My mouth felt sticky and heavy, and before long, I couldn't speak. The ground shook, and I lost my footing, and an enormous serpent exploded from the ground, growing ten, twenty, I don't know, fifty times its size. And when it opened its mouth, a woman with black hair and bird feet with long talons stepped out from between its jaws.

It was her. It was Ardat Lili."

Hannah is in tears now, and her sister is stroking her hand. Scarlet's eyes keep darting over her sister's head, looking toward the street. She looks ready to flee at any moment. I realize now she's scared of something. Or *someone*.

"Scarlet, she told me that I asked for it. That when I invited her into the circle, I asked for it. And she *welcomed* me and told me not to worry, that all I had to do was bring her the essence of men. That it was all according to her plan."

Her shoulders shake as she wipes frantically at her face. "When I woke up, my heart was racing. I was so *scared*. It was the worst dream I've ever had. It felt so *real*. And when I looked over at the man sleeping next to me, I noticed he wasn't breathing. He wasn't breathing, Scarlet. And I heard *laughter*. A *woman's* laughter. And today at coffee, I met with Violet, and she told me the same thing happened to another girl in our group. Nobody believes her. They think she's crazy. They want to call the cops and kick her out of the group. But as soon as I heard the story, I *knew*. That succubus has turned me into one of her little killing monsters, and *I killed that man* just by sleeping with him. And Jesus Christ, I don't know what to do."

I realize what I'm about to say sounds harsh, but Jesus Christ, does this girl ever need to get it together. Of all the people I could have followed today, I managed to find this absolute lunatic who thinks a bad dream caused her one-night-stand to die. I can't say for sure what happened to her fuck buddy—there isn't exactly a reaper CB radio channel or anything—but dollars to donuts his death had nothing to do with sleeping with this so-called succubus assistant. I want to curse my luck and blame the Virago, but my time might not have been totally wasted. The other sister, Scarlet, seems to be taking all of this in heroically; I don't know how she's managed to keep a straight face through all this. She's still a strong candidate for Carrie.

"You say you slept with this man, and by sleeping with him, you killed him?"

Hannah nods with her whole body. "Yes. I'm so sorry, Scar, I know you don't believe in any of this shit. I just—I don't have anyone else I can tell. I don't know what else to do."

Hannah is crying so hard now that she can barely speak. She gulps down air, choking with each breath. Scarlet folds her sister into her arms, cooing to her, calming her with kindness and love. When the two pull apart, the look on Scarlet's face is calm but dark.

"I know what you're going to do," Scarlet says softly, a slow smile stealing over her lips. "You're going to sleep with Noah tonight."

My breath catches in my throat at the unspoken implication of the plan. A murder plot! When I woke up this morning, I had not anticipated my day would grow so exciting. And while I wonder if this revelation means another raven will be dispatched to this house tonight or tomorrow, I also realize Scarlet is not a fit for my plans.

So far, I'm not exactly batting a thousand. I've found a pedophile, an aspiring murderer, a witch, and a cranky old woman with bad hips. Frankly, the entire venture has begun to put me off; have I met a single person worthy of becoming a fetus in Carrie's belly? The girl I met with the pedophile, Leigh, can't keep a lawn alive. The man who tried to shoot me out of the sky is too psychotic. Why is it so hard to find the right person in this town? How hard is it to find somebody normal?

And I'm just trying to find someone to kill. Imagine if I were trying to find a date.

CHAPTER EIGHT

October 31st

TODAY IS HALLOWEEN.

I open my eyes and blink several times before I realize the faint blurriness isn't something in my eyes; it's the city shrouded in veil. The air tastes faintly of food magic: garishly frosted sugar skulls, *pan de muerto*, caramel apples, and honey mead. I smell altars bedecked with gourds, paraffin candles, cast iron cauldrons. Even this early in the morning, the souls from the Other Side are already drifting through the veil. I can feel the vibration in the air. It's unsettling.

Today's the day.

I decided late last night as I was drifting to sleep that I need a new candidate list. To complete my quest and do justice to Carrie's womb, I need to switch it up. The hunting methods I've used thus far haven't panned out. And since the definition of insanity is performing the same tasks over and over and expecting different results, I decide my plan of attack wants changing.

The problem I've been having, as I see it, is that I was

looking for someone special amid a sea of freaks. My hometown's motto is "Keep Austin Weird," and they take it seriously. Your average Austinite is anything but average. Corporate lawyers by day are burlesque dancers by night. That kid in a hoodie and flip flops is the CEO of a multi-million-dollar startup. The old man with the pink hair is a sex comfort worker.

I've been looking for Pollyanna in a den of Lady Gagas.

So today I plan to go to the dullest, dreariest place I can think of to find the least interesting, most average people I can imagine.

I'm headed to the mall.

I'm flying over Waterloo Walk, a sprawling outdoor shopping center on the north side of the city. It's peopled by very average families doing very average things and thinking very average thoughts. I don't know this last part for sure, of course, because I can't read minds; more's the pity. It would probably make this mission easier if I could.

But anyway, if I'm to have any luck at all, this mall is the place. There aren't any hip cafés or trendy secondhand shops or live bands hoping to be discovered. The entire strip mall is a panoply of vanilla, everyday, pedestrian marks, which is good because I've officially run out of time.

Intermingled with the living, I catch sight of the dead. They drift in and among the living, flitting here and there, coming and going as they please. Sometimes they walk right through a corporeal person, and the living person gets a chill and shudders. It's fantastic to watch, especially since, to my eyes, the living and the dead look exactly the same. Sometimes, you can tell the dead by their clothing, but not always, since it *is* Halloween after all. The woman in the Victorian bustle might have died in 1842 or she might be a Java developer with a coworking space and a penchant for historical cosplay. It's impossible to know for sure. The only difference between the living and the dead is that the dead are always smiling.

It's disorienting seeing the departed at Waterloo Walk, and if I'm honest, I'm really disappointed in them. They have the chance to visit their loved ones one night a year and they choose to visit them at the mall?

Well, there's no accounting for taste. No one said dying makes you couth.

Before long, I spy a young woman with a high ponytail smiling prettily at a young man with a backpack slung over his shoulder. Either of them could be souls for Carrie, I suppose, but I don't like the way the girl arches her back as though trying to draw attention to her bosom. No, she's too self-centered for Carrie. And I don't like the way the young man tries to look uninterested in the conversation. He's too phony for Carrie.

Moving on from the young couple, I find a middle-aged woman pushing a stroller. Her face is heart-shaped and pleasant, her gait slow and self-assured. But when she passes a family speaking Spanish, she gives them a dirty look and mutters under her breath that they should learn to speak English.

Across the way, two men are sitting on a bench outside a maternity store, presumably waiting for their shopping counterparts. They do that thing guys do, where they sit close enough to hear each other but not so close that they might be mistaken for homos. They both have kind faces, but one of them is wearing camo pants, and when he laughs at the other man's joke, his shirt flap reveals a holstered gun at his waist. I can't imagine Carrie being the sort of person who keeps company with firearms. The other man, I realize now, is smoking a cigar, and I don't want to put a smoker in Carrie's belly.

I discount two teenagers vaping, a surly woman who shouts at a driver talking on a phone, a boy who hides from his mother until she's hysterical with worry, and the mother herself because someone needs to discipline that little scalawag.

I overlook a gangly teenager with sloping shoulders, a couple of women in flip flops, and a middle-aged man with a beer belly. No, no, no, and no. And as I fly from locale to locale, I realize I am inventing reasons not to take these people's lives, because I…

…am not like Grackle.

I respect them.

I don't particularly want them to die.

I *do* love them too much.

"But I have to do this," I scold myself, gritting my mandibles. "Carrie needs that baby. I need to be the one who brings it." I crane my neck around to take in the people in every direction. "Just choose one!" I say, my inner monologue growing steadily more frenetic. "That one with the pink t-shirt! No, her legs are too scrawny. That father with the bushy mustache! No, not him, I don't like the way he's eating his ice cream cone. That old man? That girl in the wheelchair? The grandmother in the sari? Raven! It doesn't matter which you choose! Take one! Any one! Take it! Do it! *Do it!*"

And with these final thoughts running unabated through my mind, I launch myself into the air to put distance between myself and those poor people, none of whom knows how close they just came to being a pawn in my game. And now I hate myself for being so depraved, for being so cavalier, for being so selfish. Was I really considering taking someone's life just to feel a moment of praise and glory from a human woman? Is this really who I am?

Yes, I think bitterly. *This is exactly who you are. This is all you are. You're a nasty, brutish little bringer of death. Everywhere you go, you leave tears and sorrow in your wake. You are nothing to be celebrated, nothing to be loved. But you have one chance to do something beautiful. So suck it up, buttercup, and get to work.*

I'm flying westward with no real destination, hoping that the fresh air will clear my mind and reorient me to my mission. The trappings of the city are thinning out—lots are bigger, trees are denser, roads are fewer, homes are becoming fewer and further between. Eventually, I see a sprawling green lawn dotted with people, and as curiosity tickles my spine, I descend to get a closer look.

In the middle of the courtyard is a complex of stately buildings; together, they look like a cross between a small university campus and a plantation. In the center stands a grandiose colonial-style building, gleaming white pillars guarding the building's austere face. A dozen windows overlook the quad, lace drapes drawn loosely against the thin autumn light that glints off the glass.

The aroma of cinnamon buns draws my attention, and my stomach rumbles. I have an unabashed sweet tooth, and anyway, it's Halloween, and I feel I deserve a treat or two. I follow the scent toward a trio of people sitting on a blanket: two women and one man. The man and woman are snuggled up together while the second woman sits off to the side. The lovers are very fond of each other: they keep pressing their faces close, rubbing noses together. They don't seem to notice that this irritates the other woman, who says nothing but looks away. I choose a strategic landing spot, close without being obtrusive, and near enough that they may toss me a few morsels. I alight and find that the grass is damp with dew.

"She's thinking about buying some land out in wine country. Doesn't make any sense. Her husband is an alcoholic."

"Pru." The man gives the third wheel—Pru—a sharp glance, following it up with a short shake of his head, motioning with his chin toward the woman resting on his shoulder.

But the cuddling woman with her head against the man's shoulder only smiles. "It's okay," she breathes, snuggling closer. "Dr. Dreeson is teaching me that my problems are not because of the alcohol. I'm not an alcoholic. I use alcohol as an excuse to misbehave." With her eyes closed, she reaches up to stroke the man's face, then lets her fingers trail down to his flannel shirt, running softly against the weft. "Did Dr. Dreeson tell you that?"

"You know the doctor doesn't give us that kind of information," Pru sniffs. "Esther. I'm trying to talk to you. Do you mind sitting up? I've brought you some breakfast."

"I already ate," Esther says. "They serve us breakfast at precisely seven o'clock. You should know that. It's in the materials. Didn't you read the materials?"

Pru rolls her eyes and reaches into a brown paper bag, retrieving a cinnamon roll. "So you don't want any of this?" She breaks a piece off and holds it out toward the other woman.

"Dr. Dreeson says I shouldn't have too much sugar. He says it interferes with the hormones that regulate my impulses." She drags a finger along the lines of the man's mouth. "But I don't have any trouble with my impulses. It's only *other* people that have problems with my impulses."

"You're not going to get any better if you don't try," Pru says, her voice thick with exasperation. "How long have you been in this place? Almost two years? It's like you're not making any progress at all."

Esther isn't listening to the other woman. "Peter, you smell good." Esther presses her face against the man's chest, and Peter strokes her head lightly.

Pru's face tightens. Her mouth is drawn into a tight little pucker, her steel-gray eyes clouding over. She drops the pastry back into the bag, brushing the crumbs from her fingers. After a moment, she pulls a cigarette from her purse and dangles it between her lips. She leans slightly forward. "Peter, I need a light."

Peter gives Esther a nudge, and though she scowls, Esther moves slightly away from his embrace, allowing him to fish a lighter from his breast pocket. He touches the tip of the flame to Pru's cigarette, and Esther's eyes follow the flame, a smile forming over her lips that gives me chills.

When the lighter is withdrawn, she burrows deeper into Peter's chest.

Pru draws deeply on her cigarette. "Esther, you're being inappropriate."

Esther's body goes rigid, but she doesn't move. "Inappropriate?"

Pru gives a short nod, a single downward motion of her chin. Smoke floods from her nostrils. "Yes. With Peter. You aren't maintaining an appropriate distance. What you're doing is too personal. Don't pretend you don't understand me."

"Peter's my *brother*." Esther's voice is thick with irritation. She bats away a wayward spiral of smoke that has invaded her personal space.

Pru flicks her cigarette with practiced elegance. "Yes. Exactly." Pru shakes her head, directs her gaze at Peter. "You just keep enabling and enabling..."

"Jesus Christ, Pru, it's nothing. We're just talking. You don't have to be big sister all the time. It's okay just to hang out. You know. Chill."

The disagreement between the siblings reminds me of Carrie, the way she'd cried when her siblings excluded her from discussing their mother. I remember the look of pain in her eyes as she'd begged them to treat her the same way they treated each other.

I look at Pru with a considering eye. Among the three, she is the outcast. Would her soul make an appropriate gift for Carrie?

I'm considering the possibilities when I'm interrupted by another bird that has just descended into the area. I turn to investigate and am surprised to see that I have been joined not by one bird, but two.

Both ravens.

The other two ravens turn bright eyes to me, mirror expressions on their faces. "You here for the job, too?" one of them asks.

I shake my head. "I haven't heard of any job here today," I say. "You?"

"Both of us," the second raven says. "And we saw three others heading this way as well."

"Three others?" I say. I can hardly remember the last time I saw so many of my colleagues in the same place at the same time.

It can only mean one thing.

"Some kind of massacre, I imagine," the first raven says. "Guess we have to wait and see. Haven't had any specific instructions yet. Just that we're supposed to come here to Soren Home."

My eyebrows knit together in ignorance. "Soren Home?"

The first raven indicates the large, white building with this beak. "The insane asylum."

The second raven clucks his tongue. "We're not supposed to call it that. It's a psychiatric hospital," he says.

"It's a nuthouse," the first bird says, nodding his head as though that settled the matter. "And that means anything can happen. Maybe a patient will hold a nurse hostage. Or maybe someone snuck a gun inside, or what if—"

"Don't be gauche," the second bird says. "People can die perfectly normal deaths even inside *mental health institutions.*"

"Normal, everyday deaths don't require a congress of ravens," the first bird replies with an edge of condescension in his voice which, I have to admit, seems earned, considering the circumstances.

My eyes flit back to the trio I had been watching before the other birds arrived. Pru is still looking off to the side, sucking on her cigarette. There's sadness around her eyes, and it reminds me so strongly of Carrie that I'm nearly sure she would be a suitable gift. Wouldn't this woman be glad to be relieved of the burden of dealing with a mentally ill sister and an enabling brother? Wouldn't she rejoice in the opportunity to start over with a mother who adores her and no siblings to look after?

Two more ravens arrive. Their landing jostles me from my thoughts, and I turn to them, frowning. "You here for the job?" I ask, though I already know the answer.

"Yep," says one fellow. "Crazy timing, eh?"

"I hate Halloween reaps," another raven complains. "With the veil everywhere, it's impossible to know if you're in the right place. All these goddamn spirits coming and going; it's chaos."

"Wasn't there a third bird with you?"

The fellow shakes his head. "Nah, he wasn't with us. Some hanger-on, I guess. God, what a mess."

"It's a right cluster," another raven agrees. "Finding the marks is such a pain in the ass with layers of veil everywhere. And once you finally get them to the Near Shore, there's all that commotion coming from City of Departures—"

"Oh, don't get me started! It's *so* hard to keep them focused! They all want to check out what's going on over there! Half the time they don't even realize they've died!"

"Yeah, agreed. It's the pits." The speaker looks around, whistles. "Five of us, then? Wow, what an event. Anybody have any information on what's about to go down? Five reapers. I've harvested five at a time before, myself. That's at least twenty-five dead, then, yeah? Wow."

I shake my head. "Not me. I just happened to be in the area. So, four reapers. Still, you're right, that means about twenty dead. And—"

My words are interrupted by a commotion coming from Soren Home. The front doors of the white-columned building fly open, scrub-clad men and women pouring out. They throw looks over their shoulders as they flee, and those of us in the courtyard follow their glances skyward. From the topmost row of windows, gray smoke is billowing into a gray sky.

"Fire!" someone shouts.

I look to my companions, whose expressions have gone dark. The lines of their faces are set; their jaws are tight. I recognize that look: I get the same way when I'm about to embark on a reap. An orange-red flame licks out of an open window; I automatically catalog it as a possible entry point. The other ravens note it as well, pointing with their beaks at the window as a series of doors fly open on the east side of the building.

The first set of ravens are clawing at the grass, excitement humming in the air around them. The second set of birds looks a bit calmer, but all four of their bodies are taut, their feathers standing on edge. More people are running out of the building, and a siren screams in the background. Then, his voice high and sharp, one of the ravens shouts. "Time to get to work, fellas!"

My companions take to the air, hurling themselves toward the growing inferno. I'm tempted to go after them, as I've never seen the inside of a burning building before. But I'm stopped by the commotion going on behind me.

Esther is scrambling to her feet, her hands wrapped around her mouth in a makeshift megaphone. "Let the motherfucker burn!" she shouts, hysterical laughter ripping out her chest. "She really did it! She said she was going to lock the night nurses in the art room and light them on fire! The crazy bitch did it!"

Her brother turns an astonished face in his sister's direction. "Who did? Somebody's locked in a room? What are you saying? We have to tell someone!"

"Ah, screw them!" Esther shouts, nearly dancing in her skin. She's laughing so hard her whole body is shaking. "They're getting what they deserve. You don't know what it's like here; you don't—"

Peter pushes past his sister, running up to a crowd of nurses that have already evacuated the building. "There's someone locked in an art room," he says, his words tumbling out so fast he almost doesn't make sense. "Esther said there's somebody still in there. Locked in a room!"

A parade of fire trucks comes squealing up the street, screeching to a halt in front of Soren Home. The firemen jump out, shouting commands at each other and hauling hoses toward hydrants. A hysterical woman is running up to the firemen, pointing to a room on the top floor. As I follow her gaze, a window shatters, glass shards raining to the ground below. Someone screams, and the onlookers cover their ears as they back away from the building.

The noise is astounding. I look around for my companions, but they're nowhere to be seen. Perhaps they have already found their entrances and are busy snapping up silver cords as I sit here and watch. In all the commotion, I have forgotten my mission.

I lift myself into the air to get a better view of the situation. The firemen have got the water on and are directing it toward the building, though it seems such a small show of force compared to the conflagration. The fire rages out of control; something inside the building is collapsing, and the ensuing groan is deafening. More glass shatters as the firemen direct the water through the doorway, into the windows, toward the giant flames that climb skyward.

The chaos is perfect. Pru and Esther stand at the edge of the green, Pru trying to console her sister who is now sobbing, screaming profanities at the engulfed building. Tears stream down her face as Pru shushes her, trying to smooth the tears from her cheeks, but Esther slaps her hands away, reaching with curled fingers toward her sister's face, scratching and clawing, teeth bared.

I could rescue Pru now. Alone in the sky, my companions inside the building reaping souls from the fire and smoke that threaten to destroy all of Soren Home, I could clip Pru's soul into my beak and release her from the surly bonds of Earth. The opportunity is here. It's now or never.

I laser in on Pru and her sister, making sure I can differentiate between their cords. The last thing I want to do is accidentally take Esther's cord. Her troubles have no place in Carrie's womb.

A rising chorus of shouting on the ground snares my attention, and I tear my eyes way from Pru long enough to see one of the firemen running toward the building, Peter trailing behind him. "They're on the top floor!" he shouts, "in the back east corner!"

The fireman shoulders his way through the other men with hoses, covering his mouth with his arm as he burrows his way into the building. Curiosity getting the better of me, I pull my wings tight against my body and take a nosedive toward the front entrance. Another window shatters as I duck inside the building. The flames have consumed the floor above me; the ceiling is falling in, black smoke and fiery embers raining like fallen stars and I barely make out the silhouette of a man dashing up the stairs. I follow him, keeping as close as I dare. Voices are calling after him, telling him to come back, that it's too dangerous, but he pushes on, taking the stairs two at a time as he ascends the staircase, the building threatening to crumble around him any moment now.

We reach the top, and the fireman stops long enough to peer through the smoke to search for the locked room. I see it before he does it; someone has moved a massive armoire in front of a door. He dashes toward the armoire, but comes up short; whoever had been in the room has managed to push the door open despite the large piece of furniture. The fireman and I peer inside. The room is blessedly empty.

The fireman is stunned only for a moment. A series of emotions pass over his face: relief, then confusion, then fear. He backs away from the door and shouts, "Die!" He listens for something, but it's impossible to hear over the sounds of wood splintering, exploding plaster, and raining glass.

Soren Home is closing in around us, and my heart is

thumping in my throat as the fireman dashes away from the door. "Die! Die!" he shouts again, running from room to room, pushing open doors and peering inside. Some rooms are empty. Others are littered with corpses.

Room to room he goes, whimpering to himself. "Die… die…die." I don't understand what he's looking for. I don't know who he wants to die. The heat is so immense that even I begin to falter, my vision swimming in and out. But something snatches me back to my senses.

It's the sound of screaming.

At first, I think it's a woman's voice crying out. But then I see the fireman in one of the rooms. He's crouched low, coughing and sputtering, holding an asphyxiated body against his chest.

I've been in this business long enough to recognize that my comrades have already been to this room. Whoever the fireman is holding is already dead. The screams I heard must have been his.

Somewhere behind us, something crashes to the ground, renewing my sense of urgency. I am not invincible, and if we linger too long, we will join the newly dead, lives snuffed out like so many birthday candles. But then, just as I'm about to make my escape, I pull up short, paralyzed by a new thought.

This man sacrificed himself for this moment. I don't know who is in his arms, whether it's a stranger or a friend. But I suddenly see this firefighter clearly: the type of person who would rush into a fire looking for survivors. The kind of person who would risk his body to mourn death. The sort of saint who loves and cherishes human life so much that he would risk his own to grant it to another.

I had planned to take Pru. I had my heart set on taking Pru.

But no, Pru's not good enough anymore. I want him. He's the one.

Like a shot in the dark, I leap into action, grasping this

hero's silver cord into my talons. I give myself no time to over-think my decision. He was too late to save this woman from a deranged person's practical joke. But he's just in time to save a broken woman from her despair. As I draw his cord upward, his soul slips silently from his body, which topples over, lying now atop the woman he'd been holding in his arms.

We disappear through the veil, and in an instant, every-thing has changed.

CHAPTER NINE

October 31st, the Other Side

THE GREAT BEYOND IS A MISNOMER. I've made it sound as though it's one giant, unified whole, but really it's a collection of smaller lands: the Near Shore (nicknamed Arrivals), the Far Shore, the Cradle of Life, and Departures are the more popular of these. There are other, smaller provinces, but I seldom have reason to venture out to them.

As a young reaper, I once made the mistake of abandoning my charge at the Near Shore without accompanying him to the Far Shore. I returned to Earth without completing the transaction, because I didn't know any better. I paid for that mistake dearly. My charge somehow stumbled out of Arrivals, where he was supposed to reunite with his friends and loved ones who had gone before, and ended up in Departures where new souls get prepped for delivery to Earth. The Virago had been furious with me when she'd found him being stuffed into a vehicle for deployment by a stork who should have known better.

I'll never forget the embarrassment I felt as the Virago

lashed out at me, hurling every insulting name in the book in my direction. It was unfair of her; my first real mentor had been a drunk who hadn't adequately trained me before I was allowed to carry my first proper soul into the afterlife. It was a lesson that wounded me for a long time.

But it's also why I know there's a way to get quickly from Arrivals to Departures. And I'm counting on that today.

The Near Shore is a beach that makes up the western edge of the Great Beyond. It flickers into view as I begin my slow descent, a ripple of anxiety coursing through my veins. This is where the rubber meets the road. All my scheming and plotting will be for nothing if I can't make this work.

At last, I reach the sandy beach, landing softly amid a crowd of newly dead. Thankfully, I don't see the Virago anywhere, and I breathe a sigh of cautious relief at my good luck. I open my claw to release the fireman's soul, excitement stirring in my belly. This is my favorite part of the journey, when the newly dead appears as his true self. Upon death, the soul sheds the clothing it died in, and it reappears on the Near Shore in whatever outfit represents who it believes itself to be. It's pretty entertaining, actually. The apparel really runs the gamut. I've seen new arrivals in everything from quinceñera dresses to scuba gear.

The fireman is dressed in black pants and a crisp white shirt. All around us, the newly dead pour into the arms of those who have gone before. Mothers embrace children; husbands fawn over wives.

But the fireman stands alone, watching.

I sidle up to him slowly, not wanting to startle him. Up close, I see that confusion isn't the only emotion on his face; there's something wistful there as well. But as he watches an old man sweep a daughter into his arms, the look on his face grows darker, frown lines forming around the edges of his eyes, the corners of his mouth drooping.

"Hello," I say.

The fireman snaps his head around, looking for the voice. It doesn't occur to him to look down, of course, so he doesn't see me. "Down here."

He blinks and balks as he realizes that I'm speaking to him. This is one of many perks of the Other Side; vocal communication between species is a lovely thing. He whips his head back to the sea of family and friends welcoming their dead home, and when he returns his gaze to me, the melancholy is gone, replaced now with something that looks like wonder.

"What's happening?" he asks.

"Before we get into that," I say, "can you tell me your name? This'll all go down easier if I can call you by your name."

The man swallows, opening and closing his mouth like a fish. Finally, he says, "Jacob."

I nod and open my beak in a smile. He returns his gaze to the people around him. "I recognize that woman," he says, his eyes trailing after a middle-aged lady with hair the color of autumn. A man and woman are embracing her—her parents, by the looks of them. "I recognize her, but I can't place her."

I nod again and take a little breath. "Jacob," I say. "Do you remember the fire?"

Jacob gives an offhand little shrug. "Which one?"

"Today's fire," I say. "At Soren Home. The..." I'm not sure what I'm supposed to call it. "...Mental hospital?"

He thinks a moment before nodding slowly. "I remember getting the call. I vaguely remember going inside..."

He has veil sickness, of course, and so the details of his last moments will be sketchy. But as his gaze returns to the woman with the autumn-colored hair, understanding passes quickly over his face as his mouth drops open into a little *o*.

"She was there," he says. "I didn't get to her in time. She was one of the ones..."

Suddenly, he lifts his hands to examine them. They all do this; I imagine they've seen it in some movie. They aren't see-through, of course. He isn't a ghost. But he's not fully corporeal, either. The Great Beyond is a strange place. Everyone experiences it a little differently. He curls his fingers toward the palm, opens them again. He stretches the fingers and turns the hands this way and that, examining. Then, dropping his hands to his sides, he turns to me and says, "Am I dead?"

It's always a strange moment when my charge asks me this, and without fail, they always ask. I still hope they're going to ask if they're dreaming because I want to see the hopefulness in their eyes one last time. But instead, some baser part of them knows what has happened, and they never look hopeful. Instead, they look to me only for confirmation.

I give a curt nod. "You are," I say. "However—"

I'm about to tell Jacob that he isn't intended to stay dead, but something else has caught his attention. I don't recognize any of the faces that have assembled here on the Near Shore, but by the look in Jacob's eyes, it seems they may be more victims from the fire. My suspicions are confirmed when he turns to me, hands spread pleadingly before his chest, and asks, "How many died today?"

The truth is, I don't know. I know there were at least four reapers present, but I don't know how many lives each took. I don't know how many families were shattered. I don't know how many brothers, sisters, wives, children, friends were left behind. I don't know, and I don't want to.

Instead of answering him, I change the subject. "Jacob, listen, we're kind of in a hurry here. You aren't intended to die today."

He flicks an eyebrow upward, his attention still drawn to the crowds before him. "A bit late for that," he says, not without sarcasm.

I shake my head and stamp my feet. "That's not what I mean. What I mean is, you're going back."

Now I have his attention. "Back? To my wife?"

At the word *wife*, his outfit suddenly makes sense. The

black slacks pressed to shining perfection. The white shirt with its high, starched collar and perfect black buttons. He's wearing his wedding clothing: tuxedo pants and shirt. That must be how he sees himself, first and foremost: a husband. The thought is endearing, and my blood surges. If I ever doubted that I have taken the right soul for Carrie, his concern for his family confirms that I've made the right choice. I smile, and he mistakes my expression for confirmation, relief flooding him.

"God, thank you. Jesus, when I saw all these other people with their families…I *wondered* why my brother wasn't here to greet me. He died about six years ago. Car accident," he says.

"We really should get going," I say. "But I need a favor."

He frowns as he digs his hands into his pockets. "What's that?"

"I need you to carry me."

One of the newly deceased is wearing a black prayer shawl. I indicate the woman with a flick of my wing. "Snag her shawl, will you? You can wrap me in it and carry me around in the crook of your arm. It isn't ideal, but it should work."

"Why do I need to carry you?" he asks, making no move to acquire the shawl.

I open my beak to explain the situation, then snap it shut again. I can't tell him about my plan. He might be the law-abiding sort, and it sure would send me up a creek if he ratted me out. Then again, he seems eager to return to his wife. If I just let him believe that…

"Those people are going to the Far Shore," I say. "In a minute, their families will leave. This here is the Near Shore; it's like a reception area to help the newly deceased accept that they've passed on. It's easier for the souls to rest in peace when their loved ones greet them. But the fact remains, there's quite a bit of terrain to traverse before you cross over into the Far Shore. And *that's* where the afterlife is. Not here in this in-between place. The old dead can't stay here long. They'll leave, and the reapers will take their charges through processing where they'll then be handed over to—what it is?"

Jacob has stopped listening to me. His mouth is working, but no sound is escaping. I look up at his fingers and see them working, making fluid, repetitive motions I recognize but can't quite place. And then I get it: Jacob is Catholic. He's praying the rosary.

Man, what a bummer this must be for him. He was probably expecting angels and trumpets and all that jazz. But all he gets is sand in his shoes and a scruffy companion. Religion sets people up for disappointment, I tell you what.

"Jacob," I say, "you need to pay attention. I know this isn't what you thought your death would be like." I point to the other dead who are beginning the long walk to the Far Shore. "They're not going to *Heaven*, Jacob. There isn't any Heaven. They're just going to the next stage of their death. We aren't going with them," I say again. "They're meant to stay dead. You are not. Don't you want to go back with your wife?"

At the mention of his wife, Jacob snaps back to me. "Yes," he says. "Please. She needs me."

I ascend into the air and nip the shawl from around the woman's shoulders. Where she's going, she won't need it. I curl the wrap over my wings as I settle onto the ground and, without asking any more questions, Jacob lifts me gently, tucking me under his arm like a football.

"Where to?" he asks.

"The shortcut," I say without really thinking it through. "We need to find the shortcut."

Jacob doesn't move, though his fingers tense a bit around my torso. "Which way is the shortcut?" he asks.

This is the million-dollar question.

Every reaper has a similar story. Years ago, when I was still young and enthusiastic about the job, I reaped a young woman from a surgical bed. I brought her here to the Near Shore, but, to my dismay, there was no family here to greet her. Instead, the Virago stood at the shore's edge, her expression all hard lines and seriousness. She didn't stop to chat as she usually does. Instead, she gripped the young woman's hand in her own and said, "Quickly. Follow me. You're going back."

Our feet had barely touched down on the Near Shore before the Virago had grabbed her and hauled her into the trees.

I never saw the young woman again.

When I'd asked the other reapers about it, they all shook their heads in wonder. "Nobody knows where the Virago takes them," they said, "but one thing's for sure. They didn't go back out the way they came. She must have taken them through some shortcut from Arrivals to Departures. It's the only reasonable explanation."

Before now, I've been satisfied with this answer. Of course there was a shortcut between the two — sometimes the dead did return to life. There have been reports of people dead for as long as five minutes before miraculously returning to wakefulness, gasping for breath to the joy and astonishment of their doctors and families.

These are the people the Virago has snatched from the Near Shore and somehow shoved back to Earth.

The question, of course, is how?

To the north, the sandy beach we are standing on thins out, becoming rockier as sand gives way to soil and eventually underbrush. From there, a path winds into a thicket of trees, and beyond the trees is the Far Shore.

Which means the shortcut probably isn't that way. But that's all I know.

"Let's try east," I say, putting as much authority into my voice as I can.

But Jacob hesitates. "If you don't know the way to the shortcut," he says slowly, "why don't we go the way you do know? It's not a shortcut if it takes us forever to find it," he says.

I sigh in exasperation. "You're just going to have to trust that we can't. So. East," I say again, indicating the direction with a tilt of my head. "I have a good feeling about east."

Jacob grunts, but he doesn't argue. It takes him only a second to begin walking, taking care not to jostle the newly arrived who are joining up with their loved ones. We slip past them as we head toward a thin line of trees to the east, their leaves the color of early spring.

We have barely left behind the beaches of the Near Shore when something familiar catches my attention. Jacob must have noticed it too, as his pace picks up, his strides becoming longer and more confident. It takes me a minute to place what's different, but then it hits me.

Car exhaust.

The scents of diesel engines and wet tar tickle my nose, and as soon as I recognize the smells of city life, I hear the sounds: human voices, hundreds—thousands—of them, for a moment distant but increasingly present. It's like soaring past a bustling gastropub just as the front door opens and a party of four tumbles onto the street, bringing the noises of the bar—the clattering of forks, the snippets of conversation, the ambient cacophony of music turned up a notch too loud—out into the light of day.

We break through the trees to find ourselves standing in an enormous city square. Streets run north-south and east-west, and at each corner, crowds of people stand chatting with each other, some smoking cigarettes, others stuffing earbuds into their ears. It's such a different sight from the idyllic beach we've just left behind that for a moment all Jacob and I can do is stare.

This is not the Departures I'm looking for.

It's the mythical City of Departures, a city that exists for one night a year to entertain the souls waiting their turn to visit loved ones back on Earth.

The City of Departures is the best of New York City,

London, and Shanghai. It's Tokyo meets Singapore meets Copenhagen meets Boston. It's all of these places and none of them, a city that stands outside of time. Dazzling skyscrapers disappear into a clear, blue sky. Raised pavilions, yellow-glazed tiles of sweeping roofs, and shining alabaster Chinese and Turkish turrets stand hip to hip with geometric, concrete hovels, flat roofs and perfectly functional facades no doubt dreamed up by some Bauhaus student decades ago. Neon signs and wooden placards butt against each other, announcing ramen stalls, arcades, opium dens, car rentals. The juxtaposition of old and new, East and West is breathtaking. Merchants stand outside their shops, hawking their wares or inviting passersby to try "the best coffee in the City of Departures!" or "the sexiest dancers on the lane!" or, ridiculously, "the biggest tuna this side of the veil!" As far as I can see and in every direction are the trappings of Earth from many different eras: midcentury diners, Victorian saloons, hyper-modern craft cocktail bars.

But if the city itself is bedazzling, the people are even more so. Styles run the gamut from smocks the pilgrims might have worn on the Mayflower to pressed cotton yukata to silk jubba and şalvar to modern-day jeans replete with holes in the knees and fade marks around the pockets. Hairstyles, too, seem to follow no specific code. But what's all the more marvelous is that no one seems to notice or care.

"What the hell is this?" Jacob asks. From my vantage point, I can't see his face, but the wonder in his voice mirrors my own emotions. I've never seen anything like it.

But it's not me who answers. "Isn't it wonderful?"

It's a woman's voice. Jacob turns, and standing before us is a petite woman with shining red hair styled in large curls toward her face. She's wearing a tailored brown wool suit with a ruffled peplum and bright red lipstick. She looks exactly like something out of a WW2-era magazine.

"This is my favorite time of year," she says, her voice light and sweet like cotton candy. "And not just because we get to go back and visit. Although I admit, I'm so *very* looking forward to seeing the children. I suspect my time for making these trips is coming to an end. My family aren't especially prolific; our line is nearly all gone," she says without a trace of sadness. "But coming here and getting to see *this* again! I'm originally from Chicago," she explains, "and sometimes, as much as I don't miss the humdrum of living, I do miss the vibrancy of the city."

She shines a smile on my charge and extends a hand. "Rebecca," she says. "And you are?"

Jacob steps forward and puts his hand in hers. His voice is a little too enthusiastic when he says, "Jacob. It's lovely to meet you, Rebecca."

I groan, eyes rolling to the back of my head. What is it with men and beautiful women? We don't have time for this; we need to find our way to Departures without being seen.

"Where are you headed, doll?" Rebecca asks.

"Headed?"

The redhead nods. "Where's home? Where's your family? You're here to pass through the veil, right?"

Jacob falters, then gives a little shrug. "It's my first time," he says. "I'm not sure how it works."

"Well, where is home?" she repeats.

"Jacob," I say.

"Austin, Texas. You?"

"Chicago, as I've said." She smiles to take any possible sting out of the reproach. "Do you have a number yet?"

"Jacob!"

"Number?"

Rebecca hrmms and taps a finger against her chin, eyes rolling slightly upward as she thinks. "You'll need a number before you can pass through. If you're headed to the southwest, you probably need to get one from over thataway." She points in a vaguely northward direction before gushing, "I'd be happy to take you if you like." When Jacob doesn't immediately respond, Rebecca reaches into a pocket and retrieves a crumpled piece of paper. "I'm number 404,594. I've got a while until it's my turn. I don't mind. Really." She flashes another thousand-watt smile.

Sensing that the situation is only getting direr, I twist and turn until I'm practically climbing up the front of Jacob's white shirt. "Jacob!"

Both he and Rebecca fix their eyes on me, the latter giving a soft gasp when her eyes meet mine. "Well, what've you got there?" she asks.

"Oh," Jacob says, as though he's forgotten my presence. "Nothing. I mean, it's just a bird."

Jacob puts his free hand underneath me and tosses me into the air. The shawl flutters to the ground while I catch enough wind under my wings to fly skyward.

But as soon as I'm airborne, I panic. I'm too conspicuous. I don't see any other birds here—certainly no other reapers. I dive back down, landing at Jacob and Rebecca's feet. "Jacob," I say, tugging at his pant leg with my beak. "We don't have time for this. We need to get you back home."

But Jacob isn't paying any attention to me. His eyes are like wild hares, darting from the gas lamps to the food trucks to the rickshaws to the—donkeys?! A herd of donkeys is braying its way down the main avenue; I can't imagine what that's about. Now, his eyes are on Rebecca's mouth, his head bent toward her as she speaks, nodding in the right places, making the right sounds at her pauses. She places a hand on his forearm. "Should we go get your number?"

Unbelievably, Jacob agrees. Although I'm tugging mercilessly at the cuff of his pants, he kicks me gently aside, following Rebecca as she wends through the crowds, sometimes stopping to stand on her tiptoes and look around. The third or fourth time she does it, a dazzling smile lights up her face. "Ah! Your line is just over that way. Come with me." She links her hand in his, pulling him close as she winds through the crowds.

Well, this is a disaster. To get a number, Jacob needs to be looked up on the registry. But of course, he isn't *in* the registry. He's not supposed to be here. And if someone figures out that an unregistered soul is flitting about the City of Departures, it won't be long until they come looking for the raven that escorted him here. And it won't take a genius to link his death to the fires at Soren Home and to the ravens who had legitimate business there. And any of them could readily testify to my presence.

I had intended to use the chaos and excitement of Halloween to hide my illegal business. But now it seems my choices are working against me.

"Jacob!" I hurry after them, my short legs no match for their long-legged strides. "Jacob, wait!"

But he's too far ahead now. I'm losing him in the crowd. My distress is turning to panic, which doesn't help anybody. I have to keep calm. I have to think.

I'm standing in the street doing just that, trying to avoid the parade of feet that threaten to crush me at every movement, when I hear a voice that sends shivers down my spine. I don't recognize the voice, but those words can only be directed at me. My reaction is so visceral that I feel suddenly ill, and as I turn to get a look at the voice's owner, my heart sinks into my feet so fast I think I might pass out.

"Raven, you sonofabitch. What you doin' on this side of the river, kid?"

Looking at me over the top of violet-hued pince-nez and sucking on a cigarette is a lanky fellow with long black hair. He's giving me the stink eye and smiling.

His name is Salazar.

The sin I always knew I'd have to answer for sooner or later.

Ten Years Earlier

"Y OU'RE MY NEW WHAT?"

The grumpy old bird glared at me through the thin morning sunlight, rustling himself out of what I assume was a deep sleep. The air was chilly, and I shivered beneath my new coat of gleaming feathers. I'd primped and preened for this moment. I was a bundle of energy, ready to explode at a moment's notice.

"I'm your new apprentice," I repeated. "The Virago sent me. My name is—"

"I don't care," he interrupted, rubbing the sleep from his eyes. "Can you come back in a few hours? I'm kind of in the middle of something here."

"Looks like you're sleeping to me," I said.

"That's right, and I'd like to get more of it if it's all the same to you," he said, snuggling back down into his nest.

I chirped, fluffing my feathers and shaking off the dew that tried to settle on my wings. "The Virago wants you to take me down to the east side. Specifically, the headquarters of the Ordo Templi Orientis. She asked me to remind you to point out all the major landmarks along the way. She says I need to know this city like—"

"Like the underside of your wing. I know," he grumbled with a sigh. "Shit. My new apprentice, huh? Guess that makes me an old-timer."

I wasn't sure if that was good or bad, so I said nothing, hopping out of the way as my mentor pulled himself from his nest with a groan. "Old bones ain't what they used to be," he said. "You bring anything to eat? I could go for some scrambled eggs and bacon right about now."

I shook my head and stamped my feet. "Sorry. I don't even know where to get anything like that. All the places I saw on my way over were swarming with grackles."

The old bird laughed. "You wanna be a reaper in Austin, you're gonna have to show those grackles who's boss. They'll take the food right out your beak if you let them. First order of business: grow some balls, Champ. Then peck those grackles right in the eye. They're gossipmongers: all it takes is you giving the ole one-two to one of their guys—don't matter how small. Won't nobody mess with you after that. You think you can handle that? Should we go practice?"

Even as a fledgling reaper, the idea of beating up grackles wasn't particularly appealing. "Maybe another time," I said, offering what I hoped passed for a smile. "So, the Ordo Templi Orientis? Where's that?"

"Other side of town," my mentor said, head cocked to the side in thought. "Weird place for her to send us, though."

I frowned. "Why's that?"

The old bird looked like he was going to say something, but thought better of it. He bided his time, scratching idly before saying, "You don't happen to know what a chaos magician is, do you?"

I frowned, shaking my head. "No. Never heard of it. Why? What is it?"

The old bird made a grumbling sound in his throat as he

thought. "It might be nothing," he said. "It's just that those folks over there—they're not like regular people. They *know* things."

That piqued my curiosity. "What kinds of things?"

"Things about life and death," he said. "Things about how to create something from nothing. Things about alchemy and guardian angels and—"

"There's no such things as guardian angels," I said with a laugh. "It's just something people made up to make themselves feel better."

My mentor eyed me darkly. I didn't like the expression he wielded when he said, "You're not ready for this. I can't imagine why the Virago would send you. This has to be some mistake."

Nothing my mentor said could have aroused me more. The idea of darkness and secrecy and learning something above my pay grade was so exhilarating that I thought I would begin molting. Which would be a shame after all the trouble I'd gone to making myself presentable.

"We should probably get going," I said, returning to the subject at hand. I didn't want to give him time to think about the Virago's request. He was old, after all—he certainly knew the Virago better than I did, and likely even had an actual relationship with her. If he thought too hard on her orders, he might decide that she needed convincing otherwise, and I didn't want to give him that chance. If danger and excitement were at hand, I wanted in.

I hadn't become a reaper for nothing, you know.

"All right," he said. "No reason to prolong the inevitable. Though I do think we should stop for pancakes. You're not gluten-intolerant, are you?"

He didn't wait for an answer. He launched himself into the sky with alarming grace for a geezer, and I followed quickly. We found a comfortable current that carried us high and gently over the city. We soared for several minutes before my mentor pointed out a small café at the corner of a busy inter-section. "There," he said. "There's a woman there who'll give us breakfast if we're early enough. You'll have to fight off the grackles, though," he warned with a chuckle. "Think you can handle it, Champ?"

"What, right now?" I stammered, eyes wide. "I thought we were heading down to the temple."

The old bird shrugged, which caused him to stumble slightly off his flight path. "The nearly dead ain't goin' anywhere," he said. "Besides, if I'm taking you down to the OTO, you better get some sustenance in your belly. That isn't the place to be off your game."

Without waiting to hear my argument, my mentor banked to the right, letting himself descend slowly until he was within line of sight of an old woman sitting outside, smoking a cigarette. When she saw us, her eyes narrowed, though her face seemed to grow pink with delight. It was hard to tell, though, as her mouth was a firm line that didn't look like it ever smiled, and her voice didn't sound pleasant when she called out, "You're back again?"

My mentor dropped to the ground several feet away from her and then calmly approached. I kept further back, wary that she might throw the still-burning butt at me. It had happened several times; once, it nearly caught me in the eye. But she merely crushed the butt against the pavement before pulling a fist-sized muffin from her apron pocket.

She broke it into two equal pieces and tossed them in our direction. With a glance at my mentor, who went for the nearest bit, I hopped toward the second before it could roll out onto the street. And sure enough, just before I could reach it, a nuisance of grackles descended from a nearby tree, making a beeline for the pastry.

There were at least half a dozen of them, and bigger than I remembered. They smirked as the largest of the pack clipped the muffin in his beak, claiming it for himself.

I almost backed away when I heard my mentor bark, "Remember what I said? Don't be a pussy."

I didn't want to cause a scene. Fighting with a torment of grackles on my first real assignment wasn't how I wanted to begin my morning. But the muffin did look delicious, and I was hungry. And if my mentor were right, I'd need my wits about me for this reap, which meant I couldn't very well go in there lightheaded and thinking about snacks. I needed to be sharp.

I needed that blueberry muffin.

Without giving it another thought, I lunged for the grackle with my muffin between his beak. I screamed as I dived into him, head-butting him in the chest and swinging for his face with my left wing. He yelped and stumbled back, but he didn't release my muffin. Instead, he lunged toward me, actually inviting me to fight.

I growled at his audacity. I heard his friends hawking and cawing for him, building his confidence and cheering his assured victory. After all, he already had my spoils in his mouth. If I couldn't make him let go, I was going to walk away empty-handed, a coward on my first day out of the gate.

I couldn't let that happen.

I issued a mighty yawp as I flung myself toward the grackle, aiming my talons for his eye. I couldn't see how well my kick landed, but as I twisted my body before landing on the pavement, I felt a tug and heard a scream. My claw had caught him right in the eyeball and gotten stuck. I yanked free, and the grackle cried out in agony, dropping my muffin on the ground. Blood spattered across his face, and his eye oozed some indeterminate gelatin. Wounded, he shuffled into the pack flocking around him, throwing murderous glances over their wings at me.

I picked the muffin from the ground, no longer hungry. There was no shine on this victory. Looking over the birds, I realized how small they were, how lackluster compared to me. I'd won, but I had size and grandeur on my side.

I was nothing more than a bully.

My mentor appeared at my side, sporting a look of grim satisfaction. "That's what it takes in this world," he said. There was no pride in the words, only an earned wisdom. "The strong and beautiful eat; the weak and profane go hungry. You're a black bird, so you can't be beautiful. So you'll have to be strong," he said. His eyes glimmered. "The world will fight you at every opportunity, Champ. Remember that."

I finished what I could stomach of the muffin before we took to the air again, my mentor taking the lead. As we crossed the city, he pointed out the highways, side roads, neighborhoods, and rivers that were part of my geographical training. We flew over Congress Bridge, the state capitol, the university. He showed me a statue of Stevie Ray Vaughn, a graffitied art wall that claimed, "I love you so much," and an eight-foot dinosaur sculpture. From our vantage point, the city was fascinating but quiet. From up here, it looked like nothing could ever go wrong.

As we crossed over the interstate, we began our descent. Instead of swooping down toward the target building as I had expected, my mentor kept an even distance between ourselves and the building, letting the wind currents carry us as we blithely circumnavigated the block. "Down there is our destination," he said, nodding toward a recently-updated bungalow with a wraparound porch, clearly not part of the original architecture. "That's the headquarters of the Ordo Templi Orientis, home of the chaos magicians."

It didn't look like much, just your average suburban home, though better kept than the neighboring houses. The grass was short and well-tended; no weeds sprouted between porch slats. A small pile of mail lay just outside the front door. But it wasn't the building's neatness that caught my attention.

The building had its own *energy* field.

"What is this place?"

"I already told you. Headquarters of the OTO."

I frowned. "But what is *that?*"

"The OTO is a magical fraternity," my mentor said. "And I don't mean stage magic. These people are the real deal."

I wrinkled my brow. The idea of humans having actual, working magic was ludicrous. I'd never heard of such a thing. "I thought—"

"Don't get me wrong, they can't levitate or raise the dead or time travel or anything," he said, "but they can do some minor things. Raise energy. See likely future outcomes. Influence the natural order of events. Things like that."

That didn't sound like magic to me. That sounded like the basics of living. As if reading my confusion, my mentor chuckled. "It's magic to them, anyway. But sometimes…You feel it, don't you? The energy coming off this building?"

I nodded. "Yeah. It feels like electricity. What is it?"

"It's a veil."

I blinked in surprise. "Already? I thought the veil only appeared at the appointed time of death, and we're—"

"It's not one of ours," he said. "They made their own."

It took a moment for the weight of those words to sink in. The implications of what someone could do if they could make their own veil hit me hard, and for a brief moment, I wobbled off course. "Their own veil? You mean the living and the dead can pass through here any time?"

My mentor shook his head. "No, not exactly. You still need wings and a beak to pass through the veil except on Halloween."

"But I don't understand. What's the point of having the veil if—?"

"You don't have to pass through to talk to those on the other side," he said. "You get close enough to the veil, and the living can have a full conversation with those who have passed on. The part I don't understand is how they remember those conversations. Everything that happens under a veil is so fuzzy and dreamlike. But hell, maybe there's no veil sickness inside a manmade veil."

I shuddered. The uncertainty felt like burrs under my skin. "That's creepy."

My mentor huffed and made a strange face. "Now, *that's* a fact. That's why I said it's strange that the Virago sent you to accompany me on this mission. Lots of unknowns. Means anything can happen. Better have your wits about you."

My mentor indicated for me to follow and we descended, keeping our distance from the manmade veil surrounding the house. When we landed, I asked, "Will we be able to shift skin inside their veil?"

"I don't know," he admitted. "Never gone inside a manmade veil before."

The beginning of fear bubbled in the pit of my stomach. Overhead, the sky was growing dark as storm clouds rolled in. The temperature had begun to drop, and I shivered against a chill that had overtaken my bones. "I don't like this," I whispered, fear making my words tremble. "Maybe we should go back. Maybe we can ask the Virago—"

"We don't back out of missions," he snapped. "You don't complete a mission, you're out of a job. It's that cut and dried. Plenty of other ravens are ready to take your place. It's a coveted position, as you well know. So if you're not up for it, you feel free to go home. But it'll be the last job she ever sends you on."

His eyes peered into mine, waiting for an answer. I glanced over his head toward the house shielded in the strange energy that made my feathers itch. I didn't like it, but the Virago had sent me. She must have had a reason for it. If she thought I was ready, I must be.

I returned my gaze to my mentor and sucked in a quick breath. Then, before I could change my mind, I gave a single nod. "All right. If you say we're doing this, we're doing this. Just tell me what to do."

My mentor grunted, a sound that I was learning meant approval. "All right. Then here's what we do."

My mentor laid out the barest of bare-boned plans, but I was too nervous to object. The creep factor was high, but truth be told, creepiness was the least of our worries. Reaping wasn't usually a dangerous game, since most humans had no idea reapers existed, let alone whether or not we were on our way. And once we shifted skin, they couldn't see us anyway, and even if they *did*, they'd scarcely remember the encounter thanks to the amnestic properties of the veil.

But we didn't know if any of that held true. And that's what made the reap so perilous.

We flew to the edge of the property. It was there that we noticed that the veil had a strange shape. It was still a half sphere, as all veils were, but this one didn't encircle the entire house. Instead, the edge of the bubble cut through the house, extending into the front yard. Presumably, this meant someone had cast the circle from a front room instead of the house's center. We hypothesized that the true center of the house must be a closet or a bathroom or some other room unfit for casting giant magic circles.

It wasn't much to go on, but it was something.

Since the back half of the house stood outside the veil, we went that way first, seeking an entrance. Thankfully, the Virago had left us the customary open window. My mentor whistled, something like a smile almost breaking out over his face. "Well, looky there. Might be we get lucky after all. Virago's definitely been here—it's not like people in this part of town just leave their windows open, not like this."

Flying through the open window, we landed in a dark room with wooden walls, cabinets and boxes littering the floor. It smelled like printer ink; I figured it for a records room or something similar. I watched as my mentor tipped his head to the side, listening. After a moment, he turned to me and shrugged. "Damn quiet. Might be nobody's home."

That didn't make sense. "If nobody's home, why—"

"Don't know," my mentor interrupted. "Just making an observation. Come on. Let's see what's in the next room."

We crept out of the office space into the hallway. My feathers wrinkled, and my skin crawled. I could feel the energy of the manmade veil just ahead. "We're getting close," I whispered. "I don't like this," I repeated.

My mentor ignored me, stepping as close to the edge of the veil as he could without actually touching it. He leaned forward, trying to look further down the hall, but it was impossible. Several doors lined the hallway, but they were closed. If we were going to venture deeper into the house, we were gonna have to cross that veil.

"You ready to shift skin?" he asked.

I nodded. "I'm ready."

"Get behind me," he said. "We'll go single file. Me first."

We stepped through.

I don't know who screamed first: me, or my mentor. But it was I who screamed last as a thin man with white skin grabbed my mentor and pinioned his head against the floorboards, the man's full weight bearing down on my mentor's body. I expected his bones to snap under the pressure as the man taped my mentor's beak shut and bound his wings. I was still screaming like a fool when the man turned his eyes on me and said, "Come near me, and I'll kill this motherfucker right now." He shook his head as I stood frozen in place. "I should have known that bitch was smart enough to send two."

CHAPTER ELEVEN

I T DIDN'T TAKE A GENIUS to know "the bitch" was the Virago. What I didn't know was how he knew he was on her shortlist or that we were coming. That is, until my eyes caught a shimmer of movement in the corner of the room. And that's when I saw her: the watery image of a dark-haired woman who looked remarkably like the man who had just bound and gagged my mentor.

It also didn't take a genius for me to realize this woman was his mother. A mother who was not actually in the room, but on the Other Side.

One of the unfortunate drawbacks of being a raven in a human's world is that we can't actually carry on conversations with you. Sure, even at that early stage in my life I'd learned to mimic certain English phrases making me great fun at parties, but I couldn't exactly ask the man in the room how he'd contacted his mother or how he'd convinced her to serve as his spy. But the *hows* didn't really matter. He'd found someone to alert him when death was coming. And my mentor's capture was the result.

Trembling, I backed away from the man without taking my eyes off of him. I tried to shift skin, but it was useless: my death shroud wasn't available in this artificial veil. Without it, I couldn't do much against him, but I wasn't going to leave my mentor alone to fend for his life. I saw the fear in my mentor's eyes when I glanced in his direction. The entire room quivered with it. I looked back to the man, who never once took his eyes off me.

"I'm not going to hurt you," he said, which was a ridiculous statement. Even as green as I was, I knew that was bullshit. If hurting me got him what he wanted, he wouldn't hesitate. "I want you to listen very carefully to what I have to say. I know you understand me, even if you can't answer. So let's set up a system, yeah? Caw once for yes. Caw twice for no. Do you understand?"

Now, ravens don't caw: that's something crows do. But we're also not stupid, and if the lives of our mentors rely on our ability to imitate our cousin the crow, we will caw until the cows come home. So I sucked up my pride and cawed. Once.

The man began to hack and cough, a thick, rattling sound in his chest. He wiped the back of his hand across his mouth; it came away bloody. A string of pink saliva clung to his chin. "Great. *Wonderful!* Ok, time for introductions. I'm Andrej Salazar. You can call me Salazar; all my friends do. But, then, I guess we're not friends, and you can't call me anything, can you?" He laughed at his own joke, which brought on more wet coughing and wheezing. "Let's get down to brass tacks. I don't want to die today. Or any day for a very long time."

Well, no kidding. I already surmised as much when he blindsided us, tackled my mentor, and wrapped him up in tape. I waited patiently for him to continue.

"But I also understand that you can't return from a mission empty-handed; that bitch will just send somebody else until the task is done, and I'm in no mood to spend the rest of my days evading death. I would rather spend those days *living*. You feel me?"

It wasn't that I didn't understand him. Of course I did. But

I *didn't* understand how he planned to evade death. Humans were not immortal. They all died. And I'd never heard a single story—not a solitary one—about anyone who had slipped through the reaper's beak. Plus, he was obviously sick. His body was little more than a collection of skin and hollow places where fat should be. His words rumbled in a phlegmy chest; he coughed blood with wild abandon. I couldn't imagine the kind of life he thought he could have.

But that wasn't my concern. I cawed once.

"Awesome. So I'm gonna make you a deal. Well, I guess it's more of a *trade*. You're not gonna take my life today. But there's a soul in it for you. I have a cousin. He's in a coma, and nobody knows when or if he'll wake up. I see *absolutely no reason* that I should have to die before he does."

Now, *that* was a twist I didn't see coming.

"This man is in San Antonio at Our Lady of Angels Hospital. His name is Alejandro Salazar. A. Salazar, get it? He doesn't look exactly like me, but all the Salazars look similar. I want you to take my cousin instead of me."

I withheld my caw. After all, he didn't ask me a question. But I didn't break eye contact. I wanted him to know that I was listening.

"Fate is coming for me: I know that. I'm on a timer, same as everybody else. But that's exactly why I think this can work. People die all the time. God, you must have *thousands* of people pouring into your world at any given minute. Surely if you take my cousin's soul instead of mine, nobody would ever know the difference. At the very least, not for a long time. Not until I'm old and wrinkled and have already lived a full and eventful life. But I'm only forty-four, you sonofabitch. It's not my time." He hacked up another clot of blood that belied his words. He pointed to my mentor bound on the floor. "You take my cousin's soul instead of mine, and I'll let him go. I swear it. You both can go. But I want to live my full life. You understand?"

I thought about this question. He didn't ask me if I agreed. He asked if I understood, which I did. I cawed once.

"Cool. One more thing. Do you know what that is?"

He nodded to the far wall, and I lifted my eyes to follow his gaze. The entire room was shrouded in shadow, but I was able to see the trappings of an elaborate birdcage. It was quite lovely for a prison: brass wires and detailed filigree. The cage was probably five feet tall and easily as wide. It took me a moment to see what was inside, and then my heart sank.

"It's a blue jay," Salazar confirmed. "Ravens and blue jays are cousins, right? Corvids. Y'all don't make good pets because you're too smart for your own good, but the jays at least can be bribed." As if to illustrate his point, Salazar stood and ambled to the cage where he produced from his pocket a collection of delicious-looking berries. He bent low, pressing his lips to the wire and said, "I *promise* to bring you your favorite foods for as long as I live. *As long as I live,*" he repeated. His lips left a wet, red stain on the gold-hued wires.

He slipped some berries through the cage, one by one, where the jay gobbled them up, never even bothering to flick a glance in my direction.

When the berries were gone, the man walked back, sat across from me. His hands rested lightly on his knees. "You already know what I'm about to say, right?"

I did. Just as jackdaws dealt in secrets and magpies in treasure, blue jays dealt in promises. A promise made before a blue jay was binding. Those vows could shift the entire universe, but they did have rules. Jays would reject a promise that couldn't be kept or that involved other parties. I could promise not to kill Salazar, for example, but I couldn't promise no one else would: that's why Salazar wanted to trade. After hearing the promise, the jay determined its legality. The sticky wicket was that you never knew the verdict until you made the vow.

I took a breath and cawed once.

Salazar leaned forward then, candlelight flickering in his dark eyes. "So what I'm gonna need from you is a promise."

I threw a glance to my mentor, who had turned his head away from me, presumably so that I couldn't read his expression or see his humiliation and suffering. I didn't want to see his wounded pride either, but I would have liked his approval and guidance, though I didn't really need it. We were both backed into a corner. All I could do was hope Salazar's promise was one I could keep.

"Promise that you'll take my cousin's soul in place of mine. Promise that you won't come back for me, not until I've lived a full life. I have *dreams*, Raven. Big ones. And I'll be goddamned if I'm gonna sit back and let this *disease* have the final say."

I wanted to respond, but there wasn't anything I could say. All I could do was sit and wait for him to ask me a question.

Finally, Salazar ran a hand through his hair and inched toward me. "You take my cousin's soul. Do your best to let him pass as me. And I'll let your friend live. You'll both fly right out of here. But if you don't come back or you take too long, I kill him. Do we have an agreement?"

What could I say? I cawed once.

The man half smiled. "Does the blue jay have your *promise*?"

I turned my head just enough to see the blue jay in his cage, eyeing me with delighted expectation. His eyes shone like liquid as he cocked his little eyebrow, his little tongue darting over the edge of his beak. "You gonna do it, my guy? You gonna promise?"

I clenched my mandibles. "You don't have to listen," I said. "Plug your ears. Don't make me do this."

The blue jay shrugged. "No one can make you do anything, least of all me. I'm in a cage, after all. You have free will. It's up to you. But make no mistake—I'm listening."

Betrayed by my own kin, I returned my gaze to the man staring at me with dark hope in his eyes. I fluffed my feathers in irritation and, praying to a God I knew didn't exist, huffed out a single caw.

We both turned our eyes to the jay, I hoping for a rejected contract, Salazar hoping for his life.

The jay spread his wings and trilled.

"He accepts!" the man shouted, nearly leaping out of his skin. "Oh, thank God! It's binding! We have an agreement! It's an unbreakable contract!" He broke down into a hysterical fit of coughing and hacking that sounded like the insides of his lungs were about to end up on the floor. The moist, slimy sound of it made me nauseated and lightheaded. When his fit calmed down, he clenched his fists and brought them to his chest. His palms were sticky with sputum. "Our Lady of Angels Hospital," he breathed. "Third floor, intensive care unit. His name is Alejandro Salazar. Bring his soul back here. You can use my veil since you won't have your own. And then I'll let your little friend go."

With one last glance to my mentor, who lay still as stone, his face turned away from me, I made the only decision I knew how to make.

I turned to my mentor's captor and cawed only once.

CHAPTER TWELVE

SAN ANTONIO WAS A MUCH bigger city than Austin, and I had no idea where to start looking. Salazar had given me the name of a hospital, but no landmarks or part of town. I had to rely on what I had learned thus far about sussing out new cities. Downtown property was expensive. Hospitals on the outskirts of town didn't help enough of the population to be worthwhile. They tended not to be too near universities or colleges unless it was *part* of a university or college, and with a name like *Our Lady of Angels,* I made an educated guess that this hospital was run by the Catholic Church, but not a school.

It took me a few hours to find the right hospital, which was no small feat. Every minute that went by was a minute my mentor was bound in tape, unable to fend for himself should Salazar become bored or psychotic. I didn't want to leave my mentor alone with that man any longer than necessary.

But getting into the hospital was going to be extremely tricky.

Without the Virago to leave a window cracked or usher me toward an open door, getting up to the third floor presented a considerable challenge. I wouldn't be able to shift skin without a veil. I had to go in fully visible, get to third floor, find Salazar, steal his soul, and get out.

I was doomed to failure from the start.

With no clear plan and my anxiety steadily rising, I circled the building a few times looking for a way in. I found not a single open window, though there were quite a few doors to choose from. I could probably get inside the lobby if I were able to somehow disguise myself.

That's when I saw a woman in the parking lot stuffing clothes from her car trunk into a large tote bag on the ground. It wasn't full; I could definitely fit inside if I could get in without her noticing.

Easier said than done.

Without making a sound, I descended to the top of a car close to hers. My mission would have been more easily accomplished in the dark; shadows would have been on my side. But I didn't have the luxury of waiting for nightfall. My mentor was counting on me. Every minute counted.

It was now or never. When she wasn't looking, I ran for the tote bag and gave a little flutter of my wings, just enough to gain some air. Then, I dropped down into the bag.

I was on top of something cold. It felt like refrigerated packaging. Maybe it was an ice cream cake. My stomach rumbled, and I chastised myself. I should have eaten more of the blueberry muffin.

I made myself as small as possible, hoping that she wouldn't look too closely in the bag as she lifted it, hefted it over her shoulder, and started toward the entrance.

I was so nervous I didn't dare breathe. I didn't even peek over the edge of the bag to see how close we were. I had to make it inside. I couldn't get caught now.

She seemed to walk for a thousand years. I had started to worry that we weren't heading for the hospital at all, that we were about to end up in a dry cleaner or a laundromat. But finally, I saw signage overhead: lots of words and arrows. Cold, conditioned lobby air and a voice overhead calling Dr. Williams to Radiology informed me that we'd made it.

I didn't move, though. I still needed to make it to the third floor. And if everything went well, presumably this woman would get on an elevator, though it was impossible to say which floor would be her destination.

Very carefully, I peeked out the top of the tote bag. I couldn't tell where we were headed, however, as I was facing the opposite direction that the woman was walking, but I didn't dare turn around. She'd probably notice that much movement, and the last thing I needed was for her to start screaming hysterically and for armed guards to chase me out of the building with batons or tasers. I needed to be patient.

An eternity later, she stopped walking. And then a minute or two after that, I heard it.

Ding.

The elevator arrived. I heard the swoosh of the doors parting. I felt the woman step inside. She pushed a button. The doors swooshed closed.

I held my breath. We were definitely going more than a couple floors. I closed my eyes and waited.

Finally, the elevator slowed to a stop. The woman exited, and I leaped up, startling her so badly she screamed and dropped the bag to the ground. I hopped free of the excess fabric and looked around. We were on the sixth floor.

I flew back into the elevator, pressing myself into the corner. I needed to stay on until it went to the third floor.

It took a lot longer than I expected. Up and down we went, picking up and dropping off passengers. Though I huddled in a corner, making myself as unobtrusive as possible, at least half a dozen people mentioned calling facilities. I couldn't leave the elevator. It was too dangerous, and I had no other plan to get to the third floor. But if facilities came to take me away, I'd have to orchestrate a way to get into the hospital all over again.

Eventually, my luck ran out. Back in the lobby, a big man got on the elevator and came straight for me. I danced away as he grabbed for me, and just then a young woman pushed her way into the elevator, breathless, jamming her finger against the button marked "3".

"I'm so sorry," she said, repeatedly pressing the "Close Door" button. "I just heard the news, and I have to get up there…"

The big man glanced from me to the woman then back to me, but made no move to attack. Probably he didn't want to upset the woman more than she already was. Instead, he linked his hands in front of himself and glared at me. We watched each other. Neither of us knew who would make the first move.

The woman alighted on the third floor, and I dashed after her. The facilities man followed on my heels, but I had the advantage of flight. I soared down the halls, glancing into open doors, seeking out a man that looked like Salazar.

As I neared the end of the last hallway, my options began to run out. I hadn't found Alejandro Salazar, and my would-be captor was catching up to me. I had to make a decision: let the man catch me and start over, or—

"Jackson! Get your ass over here already. I must've called you like three times, man."

Behind me, I heard the sound of squeaking soles stopping and changing direction. "There's a bird up here; big fucker. Bernie said—"

"Don't care what Bernie said; I need you now."

I heard cursing followed by footsteps moving away from me. My heart hammered in my chest at my good luck. I soared to the end of the corridor and saw an open door. I rounded the corner and found exactly who I had been looking for: Alejandro Salazar.

Except he wasn't lying unconscious in a coma. He was

sitting up in his bed with a half-eaten lunch tray in front of him.

And standing around him were three children and a woman.

I balked as I crested into the room. I dropped to the floor, but even so, all eyes turned to me. They stared in surprise, and I returned the sentiment, my beak hanging open in stark disbelief.

The OTO priest was mistaken. Or maybe, I realized suddenly, lying. But it didn't matter; the result was the same. He'd sent me here to reap the life of a man who might have died anyway. That's what I'd told myself as I'd hunted over San Antonio, seeking out this hospital. But this man wasn't on the brink of death. This man was awake and well and surrounded by people whom I didn't want to commit murder in front of. There were children. And if I were a betting bird, I'd say those children were *his* children.

Jesus Christ, what had I gotten myself into?

"How the hell did that bird get in here?" the woman asked, her eyebrows rising to meet her hairline. "Ugh, those things carry diseases. Kids, come over here. Don't go near that thing. Hang on a second, let me call security."

As she reached for the room phone, the man on the bed caught my eyes. He blinked once and said, "Don't."

The woman glanced up even as she dialed. "Don't what, honey? I'm just—"

"Hang up the phone, Cleo."

The woman rested the receiver on her shoulder, her brows drawing together as her lips fell into a frown. "It's not a bother; that's kind of their job."

But the man's expression didn't change as he said, "Cleo, hang up the phone *right now*."

The woman set the receiver on the cradle, worry beginning to color the lines of her face. "Is everything okay? You don't look so good. Do you want me to call a nurse?"

The man licked his lips and began to tremble. He swallowed before tearing his eyes away from me to catch those of the woman, Cleo, who looked on with deep consternation. "Cleo," he said, "I've never loved anything in the world as much as I love you."

Cleo tried to laugh, but it got caught in the bottom of her throat. She gave her head a little shake. "Honey, what—? Babe, you're freaking me out. Is everything okay? Are you—"

"I don't know how much time I have left," he said, a tear sliding down a cheek. "I want you to know that I'll always be there for you. And I'm sorry I can't stay to help you with the kids—"

"Alex, stop it, you're scaring me—"

"—but I will always watch you and love you and take care of you. I love you so much. So goddamn much."

He pulled himself from the bed and wrapped Cleo in the tightest embrace I've ever seen. He sobbed against her crown, Cleo so scared and confused she didn't know whether to hug him back or comfort the kids who had begun to whimper or to call someone for help. In the end, she squeezed him back, and when she relented, his eyes opened, and he looked to me.

"My cousin sent you, didn't he?"

I glanced around the room at the children and their mother. They were all staring at me, their faces sharing the same confusion and fear. Only Salazar knew what he was looking at. Not a bird, but a reaper. Not a raven, but an escort unto death. Without taking his eyes off me, he reached for his wife's hand and squeezed. "My cousin sent the Devil to take my soul in place of his." The woman stifled a little scream as her hands flew to her mouth, her eyes wide with understanding. He took a step toward me, getting down on his haunches to look me in the eye. "What can I offer you to send you back to Hell empty-handed?"

What could he offer me? There was nothing—nothing that I wanted, nothing that I could trade for my mentor's life. I didn't want to play any part in this crime, but my wings were clipped. I was bound by duty and honor to save my mentor, but I didn't want to kill this man. I didn't want to trade his life, which seemed full and good and wholesome, for a plagued miscreant who dabbled in magics humans weren't supposed to have. I wanted to spare him. I wanted to spare *them*. I wished I could fly away from that place and wipe this day from my memory utterly. I wished I had never heard of Andrej Salazar, of Our Lady of Angels Hospital, of the OTO, of the Virago, of reaping as a calling. I wished I could go back in time and make a bevy of different choices. I wished, I wished, I wished.

If wishes were horses.

I took to the air then, and as I became airborne, the woman began screaming as she threw her body over her husband's. "Don't take him!" she shrieked, her words almost unintelligible through her sobs. "Don't take him, please, he has a *family*—"

Entangled as they were, discerning one silver cord from the other was tricky. The children, too, had begun to wail and cry, and I knew I had to act quickly before someone came to investigate what was causing all the commotion. I closed my eyes and nosedived in, taking one of the silver cords gently in my claw.

Forgive me, I thought as I cried out and tugged.

The man's soul slipped effortlessly from his body as he tumbled face down onto the tile. His wife broke into fresh hysterics as she rolled him over, pressed her hands against his face. The children screamed, "Daddy! What's wrong with Daddy?" as tears flew from my eyes and I tore out of that room with Alejandro Salazar's afflicted soul clutched in my talons and an unpardonable sin etched onto my heart.

I flew down the hall. This time, I needed to make enough ruckus for someone to come get me, as I had no way of making it out into the parking lot on my own. I didn't have time to wait for someone else to catch an elevator down to the lobby.

I flew around, screeching and cawing my head off until

eventually I let an orderly catch me and take me downstairs. I clutched the silver cord tightly in my claw as the elevator descended. Once in the lobby, he carried me right to the front door where I wasted no time in leaping from his grasp and shooting into the sky.

I'd never flown so fast in my life. I made the long journey back to Austin, back to the OTO temple, and back to that tiny room that held the veil that I needed to pass through to take this soul to the Other Side where it didn't belong.

Andrej Salazar was waiting for me when I returned. When he saw me, his eyes opened wide, and he clapped his hands together in glee. "Jesus Christ, buddy, you did it! You fucking did it, didn't you? Can you, can you confirm or deny?"

I cawed once.

Tears streamed down his face. "Go on then. Fly through the veil. Take that motherfucker to the Other Side. When you come back, and I have confirmation that you've done what you said you would do, I'll let your friend go."

I wasted no time in transporting the wrong Salazar's soul to the Other Side. As he predicted, the two souls were close enough in likeness and kind that no one even looked at me askance as I escorted him through the Near Shore past the hugging friends and family—of which he had none waiting—all the way through to processing and finally, the Far Shore.

When I returned, the blue jay was waiting for me, his head cocked to the side. He took one look at me, and he knew. Blue jays always know. Salazar also looked at the jay for confirmation. He knelt low to the cage, pressed his cracked, bleeding lips against the wire, and said, "Is the deed done?"

The blue jay began to sing.

And Andrej Salazar began to weep in earnest.

When the weeping subsided, he ripped the bonds off of my mentor, and we flew away from that hellish place. My mentor retired after that, and I was given a new mentor to apprentice under.

I don't know what became of my teacher. But I think of him all the time.

Just as I'm thinking of him now, standing before the Salazar I wronged all those years ago—the man who wasn't supposed to die.

CHAPTER THIRTEEN

October 31st, Present Day

I ALMOST CAN'T BEAR TO LOOK Salazar in the eye. But I can't do him the discourtesy of looking away either, so I lift my gaze to meet his, hoping against hope that the intervening ten years have inured him of my indiscretion.

"I had actually started to think I would never see you again," he says, something close to a smile spreading over his face. "And now that I have you here, I'm not sure I know what to do with you."

"Salazar," I say. I hope that saying his name proves that I remember him—that our past together has not been forgotten. I'm hoping that's enough to earn me a bit of leeway. "It's been a long time."

He nods, making a strange face that I can't quite decipher. "Ten years or thereabouts," he says. "Hard to tell time in this place. You can't remember a thing on the Far Shore. All the remembering happens here, on this side. But now that I'm remembering, you know who hasn't passed through in all that time?"

I don't have to guess. I already know where this conversation is going. "Your cousin," I say, not bothering to make it a question.

"Way I see it, that sonofabitch took at least ten years of life that was supposed to be mine," he says. The emotion in his voice isn't anger, though it's not quite resignation, either. "Do you have any idea what that feels like? To know I could have had another ten years with my woman? That I could have had another ten years of just *walking around*? Hell, I could have learned Japanese in that time!" he exclaims.

His logic is flawed; just because his cousin hasn't died yet doesn't mean he would have lived this long, but I realize there's no point going down this road. "Is that what you wanted to do? Learn Japanese?"

Salazar laughs, an authentic sound with no malice in it, but I'm smart enough to know that it doesn't mean I'm off the hook. "Hell naw, what use do I have for Japanese? Point is, I *could* have. Ten years is a lot of time, friend. Time you took away from me. Time—the way I figure it—you owe me back."

I nod and wet my beak. "Listen, Salazar. You're right. I did you wrong, and I've carried that sin in my bones these past ten years. And I'm not asking for forgiveness or pity; those are just facts. But right now, I'm in something of a hurry, and not to be rude, but I genuinely don't have time for this conversation right now."

This seems to pique Salazar's interest, and the man cocks his head at me, his eyes shining with curiosity. "Well now, that's interesting information to have. Seeing you here in the City of Departures did make me wonder what the hell brought you out this way. Doesn't your business usually lie in Arrivals? What is one such as yourself doing out here?" The twinkle in his eye seems to brighten as he leans in to ask, "You got some *other* illegal business going on here, friend?"

I swallow hard in a dry throat. "Shit. Okay, yes. I'm escorting a soul who isn't supposed to be here back to the birth canals. At least, that's what I'm supposed to be doing. But the fact is, he's escaped me, and he's run off with some woman to get a number for his family visitation, and if he gets that number, the jig, as they say, is up."

Salazar strokes his chin in a gesture that looks truly devilish before saying, "If this fella gets found out, *you* get found out, is that right?"

I nod. "That's about the size of it."

Salazar smiles and does something extraordinary. He leans down and scoops me into his hands, tucking me gently underneath the crook of his arm. "Which way did your fella go?" he asks.

I indicate a direction with my beak. "That way," I say.

Salazar doesn't hurry, but he doesn't dawdle, either. He gracefully shoulders his way through the crowds, offering murmurs of "Excuse me" and "Beg your pardon" when he accidentally jostles a café table or his feet should catch the hem of a woman's dress. He's as smooth as water and fine as silk, and before I know it, we are within spitting distance of Jacob and Rebecca, who are standing in line to receive a number.

"That him?" Salazar asks when she sees my reaction to having found my charge.

I nod. "That's him."

Salazar chuckles. "No offense, friend, but there's no chance in Hell you're gonna snatch him away from that she-devil. She's a looker all right. Probably the best-looking woman in this place. That fella there probably already forgot you exist."

"Well, he might have, but look at what he's wearing. Those are his wedding clothes. Even if he forgot me, I'm not sure he's forgotten his wife so easily."

Salazar clucks his tongue and shakes his head. "You don't know a goddamn thing about men," he says. "But listen. If you need help, I'm your Huckleberry. But you know what I'm about to say next."

I roll my eyes even as my stomach turns somersaults. "You want something in return."

"Not just *something*," Salazar corrects, wagging his finger in my face. "I want to go back, too. I want my time back. So I can learn that Japanese," he says with a teasing smile.

"Salazar, even if I wanted to take you back, I can't. I can't give you back your body. I can't perform miracles. Your body is dead, buried, and rotting away in an underground coffin for all I know. Or maybe you've been cremated. Why do you want to go back, anyway? Nobody ever wants to go back for good, not that they could. Being on the Other Side is—"

"Because my woman is still there," Salazar says in a hushed voice. "And I wasn't supposed to go."

There's vulnerability in his voice, and selfishly, I feel hopeful that I can use it to my advantage. "You're right; I don't understand men," I concede. "But I do need your help. So if you'll help me with Jacob—if you'll help me get him to the birth canals so I can send him back, I promise I'll help you."

Salazar considers my offer a moment before shaking his head. "Ain't no blue jays around; promises don't mean nothing without a blue jay around. So I tell you what. I'm gonna go find me a blue jay. And you're gonna make that promise again. And then—"

"I don't have time for all that!" I cry, wriggling now to get out of Salazar's grasp. I can see the line shrinking; Jacob and Rebecca are almost to the front. "If you don't let me go, you'll have nothing to bargain with. If Jacob gets that number, I'm doomed. And anyway, in all my life, I've never seen a blue jay on the Other Side. So are you going to help me get him into the canals or not?"

The man thinks about it a moment before giving a nod. "All right. I guess I see your point. You're no use to me dead. So." He takes a deep breath and lifts me, looking me in my eye. "What are we gonna do?"

It's an excellent question, and if I knew the answer, I might not need Salazar's help at all. "You don't happen to know where the birth canals are, do you?" I ask.

Salazar shakes his head. "No. Never needed to go down there before. You?"

I shake my head. "I don't know, either. Can you buy me some time to find them? It'll be a hell of a lot easier to get Jacob out of here if I'm not stumbling around trying to figure out where to go. You distract Jacob from taking a number, and I'll find the canals. We drop Jacob's soul off in one of those boats or whatever they've got down there, and then you and I will figure out what to do about your predicament. Do we have a deal?"

Even as the words come out of my mouth, I have no idea how I'm going to fulfill my oath. But I need Salazar off my back, and truth be told, I need someone to help. Otherwise, I'm just going to wander around in Arrivals until Halloween night is over or Jacob takes a number like an idiot. So whether or not I like it, Salazar is the only ally I have.

It takes the man longer than I like for him to say, "I guess we got ourselves a deal."

I heave a sigh of relief and nod in Jacob's direction. "Great. He's getting close to the front of the line. I don't care what you have to do, just make sure he doesn't take a number."

I don't wait for confirmation. I leave Salazar to his own devices, trusting that he'll be as creative as necessary to get what he wants. I need to find the birth canals and figure out how to get Jacob inside without being noticed.

The enormity of my situation hits me hard as I realize that down here on the ground, evading footsteps and threading in and out of traffic, I have absolutely no visibility. I can't see over the humans that crowd every intersection, and I have no idea where the birth canals are located. They could be anywhere. It's dangerous to take to the sky, but if I'm going to have any chance of finding where to take Jacob, I need a better vantage point.

But just as I am about to launch myself into the atmosphere, an idea strikes me.

I could *ask* for directions.

Asking for directions isn't the worst idea I've ever had, but it's not the best, either. Asking around could still bring unwanted attention my way. If I'm honest, I can't believe I've been here this long without running into the Virago. On Halloween night especially, there are usually a thousand versions of her flitting in every direction, taking care of one thing or another. One year, there was a screw-up at the gates, and the numbers for the west coast never got called, and the dead never got to visit their families. The dead from Los Angeles and Mexico were the most furious; you can't really have Dia de los Muertos without the dearly departed.

In any case, I don't want to ask the wrong person for help, but I also can't be too choosey. What I need to do is think logically. Where can I find a person most likely to know how to get to the birth canals?

A few years ago, I was having a delicious lunch in the Greenbelt when I overheard a conversation between two women. I'm a natural eavesdropper, so I picked up the remaining bits of my meal and hopped closer to where they were conversing.

"You'll absolutely love Germany," the dark-skinned woman was saying. "Everybody was incredibly nice to us when we were there. I mean, *Disneyland* nice. A couple of the restaurants we went to didn't have kids' menus, so the waitress brought Nicole food from the kitchen for free. One waitress even sat down and fed her!"

"That's nuts," the other woman, a blonde, replied. "I guess I'm just nervous because I don't speak a word of German, and we're going to be there for like four weeks."

The first woman waved the complaint away. "Honestly, everybody speaks English, and besides, they're really service-oriented. They'll hook you up. The only time we ran into a problem was trying to get a taxi. They have super strict laws about babies and car seats. We weren't traveling with a car seat, so it was super hard to find a taxi who would take us, because they didn't have car seats, either. Eventually, though, I got smart: I looked for female taxi drivers. It worked like a charm. Every single woman taxi driver had a car seat available."

The conversation shines in my memory like a beacon, and my pulse quickens. I need to look for a matronly woman. She'll probably know exactly where the birthing canals are.

Since I'm already dealing in clichés, I take about thirty seconds to look for a yarn shop, but it's just my luck that there isn't one in sight. All right, no Granny central, but that's okay. Any place that women hang out should suffice.

I duck into the first café I come across. It's lit more like a bar than a restaurant; dim, orange lighting makes the patrons look like jack-o-lanterns. I find a bit of ledge to land on in the form of a coat rack near the door. Surveying the room, I see clusters of people: men laughing and smoking in the far east corner, a table of young women laughing over lattes in the north, a few tables of solitary men and women reading newspapers or playing dominoes. But eventually, my eyes land on her: a portly woman in her late fifties or sixties with graying hair, kind eyes, and a soft mouth. Her t-shirt says, "World's Best Grandma." If I'm looking for matronly, she's my best bet.

I drop to the floor, approaching her table quickly, and hop up onto the chair next to her. Not wanting to startle her, I wait until her eyes shift toward me before I shake my feathers, making myself known.

She gasps only a little in surprise before bringing her hand to her mouth, dabbing the corners with a napkin. "Well, I didn't think they let your kind in establishments like these," she says with a smile. "You here on vacation or are you lost?"

"Lost," I say quickly, thankful for the invitation. "I'm actually looking for...Do you know where they keep the babies?"

The woman blinks in surprise, adjusts the glasses that have begun to slip down her nose. I hop up onto her table so she's closer to eye level. "Where *who* keeps *what* babies? What are you on about?"

"The souls they move through Departures. You know what I'm talking about. The souls that become babies. Where they... you know, *get* the babies to the mothers. Where's that happen?"

The woman wriggles her eyebrows at me suggestively. "Are you asking me about the birds and the bees? You should know a little about at least one of those things."

This is turning out to be a giant waste of time. I chide myself for believing in stereotypes and gender biases and am turning to leave when the woman starts laughing, slapping the table with the flat of her hand. "Aw, come on, I'm just foolin' around! Course I know what you're asking. You want to know about the birth canals."

I breathe out a sigh of relief. "That's right. Do you know where they are?"

The woman nods. "Oh sure, I've been there several times. The babies are so sweet; I like to go down there to meet them before they get all born and ruined and everything."

This is precisely what I had been counting on, and I silently high-five myself even as I vow to be a better feminist in the future. "Can you tell me how to get there? I'm in a bit of a hurry."

The woman leans back and crosses her arms over her ample chest. "Sure, sure. Well, you're not really supposed to go down there, truth to tell. They don't like it when the babies have memories from the aforelife. Kind of wild when you think about it—our afterlife is their aforelife, and it all gets messed up. Apparently, some of the babies get really scarred from it, and it troubles them all the way into adulthood. Then they pay good money to see shrinks and talk about their mothers and get pills to feel better. But then they just get messed up again, because there's so many things to get messed up about in life. But anyway, if you're gonna go down there, you'll want to be sneaky about it. I like to go in through Arrivals."

I balk at that. "You know about the shortcut? I tried to find it, but ended up here in the City of Departures."

The woman chuckles. "Shortcuts! This place is full of 'em! You been here as long as I have, you find all the good stuff. Listen; head out to Arrivals and look for a little inlet where the water gets real shallow and clear. There's a little trail of... whadayacallit...seaweed that heads to the northwest. Follow the trail, and you'll end up at a pier. That's the canals. Betcha thought it was gonna be *actual* canals, right? Nothing over here makes any goddamn sense, but there it is," she says with a satisfied grin. "You ever wonder why the City of Departures has fishmongers in it? *Fishmongers*! Like anybody here is gonna buy a slab of tuna and take it home to the missus to cook for dinner! It doesn't make a lick of sense, but the fishmonger is always crowded."

She smacks her teeth then and gets a thoughtful look on her face. "You're smart to go down there on Halloween. Usually, that place is closed up tighter than Fort Knox. I've been escorted out of there a hundred yards before I even got to the water. Today, though, it'll probably be all hands on deck out here in the City of Departures. Did you hear they had a brawl earlier? Big one, too; I heard they had half a dozen gray humanoids to break it up. You ever seen one of them?"

I shake my head. I've heard of the gray humanoids, but I'm pretty sure they're just a myth. We don't typically need bouncers in the Great Beyond, but hell, on Halloween, I guess anything's possible.

"Well, anyway, you picked a good time. You want me to come with you? I love to buck the system any chance I can get."

The woman's discourse is delicious and dizzying, and as much as I would appreciate her company, let alone her guidance, I've already involved enough people in my crimes.

"Thanks, but no. You've been damn helpful. I appreciate it; I really do. If I ever see you around again, let's catch up over drinks." I say this last part with a wink, and the woman hoots in laughter, slapping the table again and shaking her head.

Outside, the crowds have grown impossibly thicker as more people head toward the booths to grab their tickets and secure their opportunities to visit their loved ones. Not everyone has relatives as talented as Andrej Salazar: for most people, All Soul's Eve is the only chance they get to visit those left behind. While I certainly don't begrudge anyone their opportunity to visit their living families, it does make it harder for me to maneuver.

Though it also makes it somewhat easier for me to hide.

It takes me only a moment to get my bearings and figure out which way is Arrivals. Once I'm finally centered, I take off in the correct direction, careful to keep low and out of the way. This would go so much faster if I could fly, but I've already used up what has to be a limited amount of luck for the day. It was damn lucky meeting that woman in the coffee house.

Damn lucky, indeed.

After a handful of wrong turns, dead ends, and going in circles, I finally make my way back to Arrivals. I see the Virago in the middle of a crowd of reapers. She's in rare form tonight, bedazzled from head to toe in an array of stars like the desert sky on a clear night. Her robes look like silk, colored in the shifting hues of twilight: aubergine, indigo, cinnabar, cobalt, sapphire. Over her face, she wears a rabbit mask, or perhaps it's a hare. She wears a crown of flowers glistening with dew made of diamonds, and her feet disappear in a wreath of clouds that drizzle rain. But even as I watch her, mesmerized, I note that she isn't standing still. She never does. At any moment, she's splitting into a thousand, a hundred thousand, innumerable selves, each peeling off from the core of her like a never-ending onion, each self flitting off in a different direction to perform some task or sacred duty. And each of those selves split and shimmer similarly, such that there are countless Viragos, each spreading love or fury, grief or triumph.

I tear my eyes away from this costumed Virago, hoping like a child that if I can't see her, she can't see me. I disappear into the throngs of new arrivals and their families and am soon carried down shore. I don't see the Virago here, and I heave a sigh of relief. I'm not out of the woods yet, but at least I'm granted a small reprieve.

I begin searching in earnest for the inlet that the woman in the restaurant mentioned, and as I'm scouring the jagged coast for a trail of seaweed, something in the sky catches my attention. A bird is coming into view, his wings pushing effortlessly through the veil. He crests into the Near Shore atmosphere with a handful of souls trapped in his talons—bright, undulating things glorious to look at. I know who it is instantly, and my breath catches in my throat.

It's Grackle.

He lands a bit up the coast, and due to the sheer number of souls crowding the beach, I can't see his delivery. I can't risk a run-in with the Virago, and so I wait for him to make his way further up the shore before I call out him.

"Grackle!" I shout, waving down my apprentice. "What are you doing here? I just saw you coming through the veil. It looked like you had a reaping with you."

My apprentice squints at me, licking his beak with a darting tongue, and for a moment I think he isn't going to answer me. Then, with a crooked smile, he says, "I did."

I blink my eyes. "Already? The Virago sent you on a mission of your own? I thought I was your first teacher. I thought—"

"Oh, she didn't send me," he says casually, that devil-may-care expression dancing lightly at the edges of his eyes. A chill runs through me. "I was just following in my mentor's footsteps."

I don't know what these words mean, but my intuition is screaming at me. My tongue goes dry; my blood runs cold. I am almost afraid to ask what he means. "Gra—Apprentice, what are you talking about? What did you do?"

He takes his time in answering, stroking the sand with his long, pointed talons. "You know, I was a little offended, I have to admit, when the jackdaw at the Governor's Mansion asked you for a secret, and instead of telling us both, you leaned in and whispered it only to him."

My tongue went slack; my brow furrowed in confusion. "It was a *secret!*" I cry. "It wasn't *for* God and everyone to hear! I had to tell the jackdaw, of course, or—"

"Oh, no worries there," my apprentice says, ignoring my interruption. "After you scolded me and refused to see me, I didn't have anything else to do. The Virago asked me to give you time, saying you were the perfect teacher for me, and she needed me to be patient. So I kept my distance, thinking I'd let you cool off, and then when you were ready, I would show up again, ready and eager for work. Of course, to do that, I needed to follow you. You know. To know when you were ready."

I stare at the bird for a good five seconds before I fully take his meaning. "You were *stalking* me?"

My apprentice smiles then, a devilish thing that looks so self-assured, so goddamned cocky that I want to throttle him; just reach over and choke the life right out of him. But I control my temper, swallowing down my anger as he says, "Sure did. And it's a *damn* lucky thing I did, too, because honestly, I was beginning to get a complex about myself. Beginning to wonder if I had the chops. You know, you really did a number on me, all that guilt you gave me about respecting life and everything. For a moment there, I actually thought you believed it. Which made me really question myself."

I say nothing, merely stand there like a moron waiting for

Grackle to continue. "I became a reaper because I enjoy death," he says simply, taking small, calculated steps closer to me, lowering the volume of his voice as he draws nearer. The intimacy of it is enough to make me recoil. "I *like* killing. It's what I've always wanted to do. I've never wanted to do or be anything else. So when you said we were supposed to show this reverence for life, that we were supposed to see life for the glorious gift that it is, I wondered—what's wrong with me, then? Because I don't see life that way. I don't think it is some wonderful gift to be venerated or appreciated. It's just a thing that happens through random happenstance, and it's my job to put an end to all that shit when the time comes. Death is my job. It's my reason for being. And you made me think that was wrong. And then I followed you."

I start feeling sick. I know where Grackle is going with this, and I shake my head, a moan escaping my throat. "No, no, you don't understand, you don't know what you saw—"

"I gotta hand it to you, Teach, you had a *fucking great secret!*" Grackle says with admiration. "I saw you go into that building and take that fireman's cord even though it was clearly not intended for you. I saw you reap a man whose life was not yours to take, and I saw you do it with diligence and determination and not a *modicum* of guilt. And that's when I realized, this whole time, you've been holding out on me. You've been making me think there was something wrong with me when you have the same impulses. You're not any better than me. You're *just like me*. And so, I thought, hell—if my teacher can do it, so can I."

Every process in my body stops dead in its tracks. My blood freezes. My heart stills. My mouth turns dry as desert sand. My stomach clenches and the words scratch against my throat as I ask, "What did you do?"

I follow his gaze to a group of five costumed children huddled near the front of the Near Shore. They have bags of candy gripped in their little hands. It's funny how children never shift skin: they have no idea who their true selves are, so they just appear in the clothes they died in. One is a ballerina, her golden hair coiled into a topknot held in place with a little net. One is an astronaut, one a zombie, one a genie, and the last a skeleton whose face makeup has rubbed off along his chin. He looks like he's been crying.

They look dazed, sharing the same expression as many of the people who come through the veil. My eyes go immediately to the crowds of families that have amassed just a little further on, trying to make out which people are here for these children, but none of them seem to be making their way toward them.

And that's when I understand. "No, you didn't," I say, a dark chill overtaking my bones. "Please tell me you didn't reap these children for the fun of it. Please tell me these children were tagged. Tell me it was dark, and they crossed the street without looking, and they weren't wearing reflectors..."

Grackle shrugs, that sly smile curving over his face. I see now that there's a smudge of face paint on his cheek; the skeleton's cord must have been attached at his chin. It explains the smudge. And suddenly I can't help myself from letting out a scream. "You *monster!* What were you *thinking?* They're just *children*, don't you understand? *Children!* And you took *five* of them? We have to send them back! Jesus Christ, Grackle, we have to send them *all back!*"

If I was worried about getting Jacob back to Earth before, all those concerns have fled. I can worry about Jacob later; right now, the only thing that matters is getting those children back to Earth, back to the lives that stretched out in front of them before Grackle and his insane sense of entertainment intervened. I can't imagine a scenario where five children would miraculously return to life, but that's someone else's problem.

I don't know how much time I have left. I fly to the children, squawking and crowing for their attention. They turn their wide, scared eyes to me, their faces covered in smeared makeup and masks turned askew. Dressed in their Halloween costumes, they resemble a tiny band of ragamuffin hobgoblins. My heart drops out of my stomach.

"Come on, kids," I say, flapping my wings wildly. "Follow me. Hurry up now. We have to get you back to your mommies and daddies. We have to—"

"It's too late for that, *Mentor*," Grackle laughs raucously, spittle flying from his beak. "They've been dead for at *least* ten minutes. If you take them back now, they'll just end up back here, maybe tomorrow, maybe in a week. They're gonna be *brain dead*, you moron. If you take them back now, it's worse than letting them go on."

Grackle's words are like knives in my skull. I don't know how long the children have been dead, but if it has been that long, their bodies will almost certainly reject their souls, and my returning them will do nothing but bring more misery and grief to families who are certainly already buried underneath a mountain of sorrow.

All I have is Grackle's word for it, though, and he's proven that he's a psychopath. I can't trust anything he says.

The only person who can help me now is the very person I most desperately don't want to see.

The Virago.

Ignoring Grackle, I motion for the children to follow me. Running, their little bodies scarcely able to keep up with me, they follow me through the crowds. I see the Virago up ahead, and the glimmering, shifting sight of her fills me with both hope and dread. I cry out to her, flapping my wings as wildly as I can to attract her attention. "Virago! Help! Please help!"

She scarcely lifts her eyes to me, but one of her multitudinous selves peels away from the self I'm interacting with and gathers the children together, putting her arms around them. I can't hear what she says as that version of herself leads them away, back the way we'd just come. She's taking them deeper into Arrivals.

I shake my head wildly, my pleas loud and desperate as I beg the Virago still standing in front of me, her eyes full of pity and resolution. "You can't take them back there," I say. "They're not supposed to be here! Grackle—it was Grackle, he—"

The Virago looks sad and somber, but she makes no motion to intervene. She doesn't even look surprised, and her eyes do not search for my apprentice.

I try again. "They're just *babies*. You saw them. They can't be any older than five or six, Virago. Please. Take them back to Earth. I've seen you do it before. Please."

The Virago's expression is soft when she says, "There isn't anything even I can do now, my old friend."

"Reincarnate them at least!" I shout. "You can do that much, right? Send them to the birth canals! It won't be the same, I know, but at least—"

"Raven," she says, her interruption slicing through my words like summer sunlight through a thick fog, "we don't do that. You *know* that. We're not a recycling facility. Except in rare cases, the souls that come through here are here to stay forever. There isn't anything we can do for those children. Let them go in peace."

As I open my beak to protest, she has already turned away from me, giving herself over to some other business—to some other outcome she can actually affect.

Alone, I stand in Arrivals, shame and sadness rooting me to the sand, tears brimming in my eyes.

In my own selfish desire to bring life and experience the joy of giving instead of taking, I have caused these children to be torn from the lives that were due them. And now, there's nothing more that can be done.

CHAPTER FOURTEEN

I ALMOST DON'T HAVE THE FIGHT left in me to deal with Jacob. After what I've just seen, I'm tempted to give up and let Jacob bury his memories and create a new existence here in the afterlife where he does seem genuinely happy. But then my thoughts drift back to Carrie, screaming and crying, begging me for one last chance for a child.

Indecision roots me to the spot. My dogged determination to be Carrie's hero is what drove me here; it's the root of my pain, my humiliation, and my anger. If I hadn't been so blinded by my need to rescue her from darkness, those children would still be alive, and maybe I would have had time to unmask Grackle for the monster he is. I could end all of this now, forget I'd ever met Carrie or Jacob and simply return to Earth and do the job I have been assigned.

But I've already come this far. If I stop now, those kids will have died in vain. Not that bringing Carrie a child will bring them back, but at least something good will have come out of my recklessness.

Resignation takes over, pulling me back into the City of Departures. I no longer feel panic or urgency, though. I no longer care what happens to me; I'm in this for Carrie. For those kids. I'm in this so that I can sleep tonight believing those deaths meant something.

A bar on the corner is advertising shots of Jägermeister. A trio of young men who, judging from their parachute pants and feathered hair, died sometime in the eighties elbow through the crowd, failing to crush me underfoot only because I jump out of the way, cursing as I do so. And then it occurs to me: I don't care about being seen anymore. The Virago already knows I'm here. So I launch myself into the sky to get a better view of the busy streets below.

I should have given Salazar a rendezvous point. Christ, I'm bad at this! How stupid! How am I ever going to find them in this massive city? They could be anywhere—indoors or out. And if they're indoors, my chances of finding them are nil.

But I'm not running on absolutely no information. Where had the woman said she was from? *Chicago*. If I'm not mistaken, the Departure gates are arranged by geographic location. And if I'm right about men in general and Jacob in particular, he and Salazar are entertaining a lovely redhead waiting her turn to press through the veil somewhere near the gate for Chicago.

I head toward one of the dozens of monitors announcing which platforms contain which gates, and look for Chicago. My eyes jump to the C column, skimming through the list of city names: Chesterfield, Chesterton, Chestnut Ridge, Cheval, Cheverly, Cheviot, Chevy Chase, Cheyenne. Then I see it: Chicago, platform 87, gate 16B.

Checking the map, it looks like platform 87 is west, so I fly that direction while I search the crowds for my targets. From this vantage point, the City of Departures looks truly magnificent. The amalgamation of the most endearing innovations of various times in history is glorious to see. Horse-drawn carriages clatter down cobblestone streets carved in the scant spaces between bullet-train tracks. Burlesque bars dot the side-walks, interspersed with flower shops, bakeries, tobacco parlors, and libraries. Giant hanging banners flutter on the scant breeze, announcing the salons, eateries, and boutiques in the high-rise buildings they guard. Neon café signs hum to life as the gaslight posts on the street corners gently incandesce. There's no need for illumination, as the sky is still bright blue, but the humans enjoy these things. The City of Departures is entirely constructed of favorite memories, a way to connect human souls with the lives they've left behind. It jostles their memory and reignites a long-since-lost desire to return to a world of strife, hardship, and labor. They don't have any of that on the Far Shore, so getting them here requires all the delights they enjoyed in their corporeal lives.

I pass a park with a candy-colored carousel and a giant Ferris wheel before I see the sign indicating platform 87. I swoop lower, following the signs toward gate 16B, craning my neck side to side, checking for red hair or a fellow wearing purple-tinted lenses, as Jacob's face has already begun to fade from my memory. This is a development I hadn't counted on — ravens are gifted at facial recognition, but the day's events are obviously wearing on my nerves, rendering me less than one hundred percent on my game.

I hear a peal of laughter and follow the sound to find Salazar standing on a chair outside of a movie theatre, juggling what looks like three bottles of champagne. Jacob and Rebecca are standing on the sidewalk watching, Rebecca laughing and clapping while Jacob looks on with only a faint look of grudging amusement on his face.

"Took you a lot longer than I thought, friend!" Salazar shouts, and I realize he's talking to me. "Tried to make myself as obvious as possible for you to find, but next time let's plan this a little better, yeah?"

With a sigh of relief, I land on Jacob's shoulder. The man jumps a mile, giving a little screech that makes Rebecca laugh, her head tossed back, shoulders shaking. "Your friend is back."

When he realizes it's just me, Jacob blows out his cheeks,

gives his head a shake. "Looks that way," he says. He takes a step away from Rebecca to tell me, "I thought I got rid of you."

"You're going back," I say, my voice flat. I can tell that the City of Departures is working its magic on him, though not in the way it's supposed to. It's supposed to ignite nostalgia that makes it easier for the dead to visit their families. And it does work that way on the old dead, those who came from the Far Shore. But Jacob is an abomination, and so it's making him want to stay. "I'm done listening to your objections. Were you sick when you died? Old? Anything like that?"

Jacob sucks in a breath. "No, I—"

"And don't you have a wife? Family? People who are gonna be devastated at your untimely demise?"

Jacob licks his lips, his eyes darting back to Rebecca. A cloud passes over his face, and he glances down at his hands, at the ring on his left hand. "I have a wife who will miss me very, very much," he agrees.

"Then we've got to go back," I say. I note the look of regret in Jacob's eyes, and I sigh. "You haven't been dead long enough," I say. "You haven't been to the Far Shore, so this place must be enchanting to you. It's like Earth, but a thousand times better. But here is a fantasy, Jacob. It's all an illusion. It's not real. You couldn't stay here even if it was your time to die. You'd pass on to the Far Shore, and you wouldn't remember your wife at all, not until she joined you. But *she'd* remember *you*. All the years she has left on Earth, she'll spend without you. Unless we get going. Right now."

I no longer feel guilty at the ruse. I'll say or do whatever it takes to get this soul into Carrie's womb. Jacob throws one last look at Salazar juggling champagne bottles before turning toward Rebecca. "It was great to meet you," he says. "But I gotta go."

She nods, her eyes showing only a hint of sadness. "I know. I hear you're going back. Good for you; I didn't think that was possible. I hope you're happy down there. If you remember me when your time comes, come find me." She leans in and kisses him lightly on the cheek before slipping into the crowd and disappearing from sight.

Before we turn to head back, Salazar appears at our side, champagne bottles nowhere to be found. "You weren't gonna leave without me, were you?"

I shake my head. "I wasn't going to wait for you, but I wasn't trying to intentionally ditch you if that's what you're asking. Now, let's get a move on, fellas. Time's wasting."

Perched on Jacob's shoulder, I guide him with landmarks and shouted directions the best I can, and we wend through the spidery streets, passing massage parlors, palmistry tents, and marionette stages. As we pass a patisserie with an open-air front, I see Salazar swipe a pastry from a table, dropping it into a front pocket with a practiced quickness and grace that tells me he did this often and well in his life on Earth. There's no need to steal anything in the City of Departures; everything exists for the taking. But some habits die hard, I suppose.

At long last, the crowds thin as we edge to the outskirts of the city, pavement giving way to grass, then sandy beach. "We're almost there. The canals are just a quick jaunt past the Near Shore, and—"

"This is as far as I go," Salazar says suddenly, drawing to a quick halt, inching away from the sandy shore. "I have no desire to go through Arrivals. All that hugging and kissing and whatnot. You'll recall I didn't have any of that."

I quirk an eyebrow at him. "That was ten years ago," I say.

"Doesn't mean I'm not still bitter about it," he says.

At first, his words confuse me, but little by little, I come to understand. On the Far Shore, the deceased remember nothing of their lives. The whole point of the place is whimsical amnesia. Then, one night a year, the dead are encouraged to drift from their cozy ignorance to mingle in the City of Departures, which makes them remember.

Right now, I see the darkness hovering over the contours of

Salazar's face, a glow in his eyes that looks less like the fire of life and more like the fury of betrayal.

I need to end this farce. And quickly.

"We're going," I say. "But I'll be back. I promise." In Jacob's ear, I whisper, "We need to hurry. Go."

Jacob follows the same path I took earlier, only taking a few mis-turns here and there. We backtrack quickly, getting back on course, and before long, we arrive at the piers. As far as the eye can see, small, wooden docks line the shore, each with a small vessel at its side, rocking gently on the waves that lap delicately at the beach.

Jacob halts as I take to the air, the smell of seafoam and salt filling my nostrils. I don't know where to go, but up ahead, I see a gathering of storks, and my confidence returns. This must be the right place. If I play it cool, I'm sure I can convince one of them to tell me what to do.

I approach the nearest pier with Jacob following close behind. At the end of this pier is a single stork, a grim expression on his face, brows drawn together in concentration. When he hears us approach, he glances up and his consternation deepens.

"You're not supposed to be here," the bird says, eyes narrowing with suspicion. "This is Departures, not Arrivals."

"Yes," I say, pulling myself to my full height. I make my expression as pleasant and lighthearted as I can manage. I glance to Jacob, who, to his credit, is doing the same, all bashful smiles and snow-white teeth. "I recognize that. Very different scenery. Quite lovely," I say.

The stork grunts and looks away from me, focusing on the little boats that bob gently on the water. "It is lovely, that's true. I've worked these shores for the past fifteen years. Watching the sun set over the ocean never gets old." His eyes drift upward, catching the horizon. I see the reflection of the sun and sea in his liquid brown irises. "Bet you don't have anything like this in Arrivals," he says.

"Nothing like this," I agree. I clear my throat and press on while I've got the stork in a pleasant state. "I am curious, though. I know quite a lot about death. But I'm not sure how birth works."

The stork snorts, gives a toss of his fine head feathers. "*Birth*. What messy business. We don't fuss with that too much; leave that to the women themselves. Here we just put the Potentials in their baskets. When the mothers conceive, the souls are waiting. The rest is up to them," he says.

Potentials. It's such a lovely way to describe the new souls that for a minute, I forget my mission and am lost to a fit of fancy. But then I hear Jacob clear his throat, and I shake my feathers and resume my line of questioning. "Right. Well, this fella here would like to visit with one of the, uh, *Potentials* if that's okay. Got taken before his kid was born," I say, putting an extra bit of sympathy in my voice. "I know it's not strictly allowed, but—"

"Not strictly allowed? It's strictly *forbidden*," the stork says, his cheeks beginning to color. "You know how much damage you can do to a Potential by giving it even a *glimpse* of death? These souls are innocent. You better not get any funny ideas about messing around with them." He glances at Jacob and adds, in a voice not devoid of tenderness, "Even if this fella here is the daddy," he says.

"I know how serious my request is," I say, taking a step toward the stork, his white feathers gleaming pearlescent in the sunlight. Compared to him, I feel so small and dirty, so mundane and grotesque. I feel the shame reflected in his expression, which has congealed into something close to disgust at my closeness. "Look, normally, I wouldn't even ask. Certainly not. It's just that, they tried for so many years to have a baby. And then she finally conceives, and he dies, and…It's one thing to die and leave your wife behind," I say, keeping my voice low. "It's another thing to die without ever knowing the child you tried so desperately to give the woman you love."

I'm afraid I've overplayed my hand when the stork's frown deepens. But suddenly, he gives a resigned shrug and waves his wing. "I never saw you here," he says, flicking his eyes toward Jacob. "And when I make my way back this direction, I expect you'll both be gone. And I *never*, and I mean *never* want to see either one of you again."

I bob my head up and down so hard I feel it might snap off my neck. "Never again, you got it, I promise. We won't be but a moment. But if you'll indulge me this one last question…?"

His irritation is evident as he snaps, "You want something *else*?"

"It's just that I have no idea how this works. I know the mother the Potential is intended for. So how do I…?"

"Envision her," the stork says, already turning away from me, heading in the opposite direction. "The magic takes care of the rest."

Once the stork is out of earshot, I beckon for Jacob to approach. His footsteps are uncertain as he approaches the little vessel floating on the water. I point to the little boat and say, "When I tell you to, you need to get in."

"In *that*?" he nearly screeches. "I don't want to be difficult, but I don't think I'll fit."

I have to agree that the boat is terribly small—infant size, naturally. But this has to work.

"It's probably a lot bigger than it looks," I say with extra conviction in my voice. "In this place, nothing is what it seems. After all, you don't *really* have a body. You aren't *really* standing here. You weren't really watching a man juggle champagne bottles in the City of Departures. It's all real and not-real, you get me? So you'll fit. I think."

Jacob frowns, shaking his head. "I don't like it. This can't be right. How's this gonna get me back to my wife?"

"Jacob." His eyes lock on mine, and I give him the most severe glare I can summon. We're running out of time. "You have to trust me." *Even though you shouldn't.* "Don't you want to go back?" *Even though you're not really going back.*

He nods. "I do, but—"

"Then when I say so, *get in the boat.*"

I close my eyes, turn my back, and sit, which cuts off any objection he might have uttered. Then, with his voice quiet and my heart fluttering, I conjure an image of Carrie with her wild, copper hair and her bright eyes. I see Carrie on her hands and knees, sweating and crying, giving birth to a dying child. I see Carrie in prismacolor, bright and screaming and wondrous, a potential virago in her own right. I see Carrie shrieking at her brother and sister, Carrie mourning all the wrongs life has done her. Behind me, I hear Jacob give a little gasp, and when I open my eyes, I see that the boat has suddenly filled with a bright, white light.

"Oh my God," he whispers, taking unconscious steps toward the little boat. "That light. What is it? It's the most beautiful thing I've ever seen."

I give a little nod, swallowing down my own excitement. "It really is extraordinary," I say. "And that's where you need to go, Jacob. Get in the boat. As the stork said, the magic will do the rest."

He turns to me, his eyes soft, his expression peaceful. A small smile curls over his lips as he says, "I guess this is good-bye, then."

I nod. "I wish you long life, Jacob. Now, get in. Hurry."

With a final nod, Jacob drops down to a seated position, feet dangling over the pier. He puts one foot inside the boat. He balances there, expecting the vessel to sink or tip over, I can't tell, but when nothing happens, he puts his other foot inside and lowers himself in.

And then, in a flash, the boat is filled with blinding, prismatic light in every color of the rainbow.

It's so stunning and so surreal that my heart catches in my throat as I gaze down into the little vessel. And I see there, impossibly, a naked Jacob, devoid of any defining features except his kindness and gentleness and goodness radiating off of him in waves, and I know it's him, curled into a fetal position, floating amid the iridescent rays of light emanating from the little boat.

Holy shit on a stick, I've done it.

I have to contain myself from screeching. Thunderous heartbeats deafen me to the waves lapping against the pier, breaking on the shore. I don't even hear my own wings as they beat at the air, carrying me up into the sky, higher and higher as this transformative glee fills me up and permeates my body. I am so suffused with pride I can barely contain myself. *I did it!* Oh, but this is amazing. This is *everything*. I've done it. *I've brought Carrie a baby.*

I'm so happy I soar in circles, laughing and singing out with all my might. It doesn't matter now who sees me. It doesn't matter now what happens. I've done it. I've won. I've broken through the barriers that prevent meager, hideous little me, courier of death, from experiencing the ecstasy of creating life. I am the first of my kind to have done it. They'll write songs about me. They'll remember me for eternity. I've done something no other raven has ever done.

I take one last moment to admire the shining vessel that rocks on the waves before gliding back toward the Near Shore. This delicious feeling of magnificent accomplishment stays with me as I fly. My task is complete; now, she must do what all mammals must do to coerce a child into their wombs. And this time, a soul will be waiting. And it will fill her up. And it will bring her a lifetime of happiness. And I will not take it away.

I crest into Arrivals, still high on my victory when I hear a familiar voice grunt, "Took you long enough. I was beginning to think you were trying to renege on our deal."

Salazar is crouched low on his haunches, his head cocked to the side. I open my beak to apologize, but then I stop. He doesn't seem to be talking to me; his attention is turned the other way. I can't imagine who Salazar would be talking to like that, but then, as I'm about to show myself, I see Grackle standing just a few feet away. Salazar's attention is on him.

My apprentice's chest is puffed out as he strides toward Salazar. No, not strides—he's *strutting*. The little bastard is so proud of himself that he doesn't notice how tightly Salazar is wound. Nor does he wonder why Salazar is talking to him in the first place.

"I'm ready to go back, now," Salazar says, his voice rimmed with a drunken fervor I hadn't noticed before. The effects of the Near Shore are rubbing away the protective forgetting that has kept him safe and happy these past ten years. "Time to give me back what you owe."

But my apprentice guffaws, stepping closer to Salazar. "Owe? Shit, I don't owe you anything," he says. "Once dead, you're dead. Accept it. Deal with it. Don't whine to me—"

It happens so fast. Salazar screams and lurches forward, catching Grackle by a wing mid-air as he tries to leap away. His bony fingers lock around Grackle's upper body, his knuckles shining white and bloodless. Grackle cries out in pain or surprise or both, writhing in Salazar's hands as he screams, "Get off me, you asshole! Let me go, you dead piece of—"

Salazar's thumb and forefinger wind around Grackle's neck, pressing his head in an unnatural direction, and I catch a glimpse of white greasepaint that has rubbed off on Grackle's cheek.

White greasepaint from the child dressed as a skeleton. The child Grackle took.

Shit! My insides are screaming in my head, my internal voice so loud I feel my eardrums will burst. *Salazar thinks Grackle is me. Oh shit, oh shit, oh shit!*

Salazar's right hand slides up Grackle's torso, his fingers moving under his wing. He increases the pressure, and I hear Grackle's tendons tear with the strain.

In an instant, I know what Salazar is about to do. I dive down toward them, willing my body to move faster than physics allows as I scream, "NO!"

He has Grackle's wing firmly in his hand. And then, teeth bared, he yanks his arm down in one swift movement, ripping Grackle's wing from his body.

The scream that issues tears through me like a serrated blade, slicing through my heart to my stomach. The white-hot pain of Grackle's agony explodes in my bowels, turning them to water.

"If I'm not going back," Salazar snarls, tossing the wing to the ground, "neither the hell are you." He transfers the position of his hands, and just as swiftly, rends Grackle's other wing from his body.

My apprentice bleats like a lamb at the slaughter as gore and viscera explode from the wound, coating Salazar's hands and soaking into the sand beneath them. All around us, the newly dead are screaming and running, other reapers screeching to each other, trying to corral their charges and understand what's happening. Feathers fly in the air, drifting slowly down as Salazar drops Grackle's ruined body into the blood, wiping his soiled hands against his pant legs. Grackle's feathers stick to the webbing between Salazar's fingers. "That's what you get when you break promises!" he screams. "You promised I could go back! You promised!"

As Salazar stands screaming over the pool of gore at his feet, two gray, man-shaped creatures materialize at his side. They're identical and faceless, two hulking beings that clasp their hands around Salazar's arms and drag him away from the carnage as though he were a rag doll. Salazar doesn't resist, only continues screaming about promises of going back, occasionally crying the name of a woman. Eventually, the gray humanoids and Salazar vanish from view, leaving me alone with my apprentice, dying at my feet.

"Grackle," I whisper, lowering myself to meet his gaze. My

apprentice has lost so much blood, his face has grown pale, his eyelids fluttering, eyeballs rolling in their sockets. His beak tweaks and jitters as he tries to speak, the vocal cords in his neck straining with the effort. A small sound escapes his throat as his gaze struggles to meet mine.

"Mentor," he says, blood seeping out of the terrible clefts where his wings used to be. I can scarcely bear to look at him. He looks like the ravens at the Duval house, wingless and locked in cages. But Grackle isn't going to endure the same fate. I can already tell that he doesn't have much time left. "Please, help me," he sighs, his voice ragged and cracking. "Please —"

"Oh, Grackle," I weep, stepping close enough that my feet track through his blood, the iron stink of it filling my nostrils. I lean forward, close enough to feel his dying breath against my face. "Why did you have to kill those children? If you hadn't done that, you wouldn't be dying now." I hang my head, a tear sliding down my beak. "I could have trained your killer instinct out of you. I could have taught you to value life. I could have taught you —"

"Value life?" he tries to laugh, but it comes out as a weak susurrus. "Like you do? You traded five for one."

I want to object, to counter that his choices were not my choices, that I traded *one* for one. But for some reason, even that logic is cold comfort. I sniffle and sigh. "I didn't want this for you, Grackle. This ending wasn't in my heart. But I don't know. Maybe it's what you deserve."

I back away, blinking away the remaining tears that try to form in my eyes. Grackle coughs and strains, his broken body shuddering with the effort. I watch him until he takes his final breath and his eyes cloud over, his body finding stillness. And then, just like that, he's gone.

In time, I will find space to mourn Grackle and process my part in his death. But not now. If I hurry, I can make it back to Earth before the end of Halloween. I can locate Carrie and find a way to convey to her what I've done. After the day I've had, I need to see the rapture on her face when she realizes a soul is waiting for her. I need to feel her gratefulness and love radiating toward me. I need that positive emotion to wash over me, to make me forget Salazar and the children and my apprentice and what I've had to endure today. I need redemption. I need praise. After everything I've suffered, I think I've earned it.

CHAPTER FIFTEEN

October 31st, Austin

BY THE TIME I RETURN TO AUSTIN, the sky has begun to grow dark, porch lights and street lamps flickering on, jack-o-lantern flames glinting in the soft darkness. The city smells sweet and welcoming, like candy apples and dew on freshly-cut grass. Front doors open, and groups of trick-or-treaters in various degrees of costumed finery trickle out with laughter and screeching. Parents amble behind their charges, chatting with neighbors and calling for their overly ambitious ghouls and goblins to hold on and not to cross the street without looking both ways. The children whine and run; the parents sigh and scurry to catch up. The moon offers gentle light to guide them, washing them in its silvery rays.

I make my way towards Carrie's house by pure memory. I recall a line of trees, vintage cars, the shape of hills in the background. I remember a school nearby and a bakery on the corner. Of course, that's not terribly much to go on. But somewhere in the annals of my heart, I feel Carrie etched inside me, and I decide to turn off my chattering brain and just follow the beats wherever they lead.

Down below, children are crossing the street, running up to a house with no lights on. It's against the rules, of course; if a house doesn't have lights on, it means they don't want to be bothered. But these kids are young; no one has taught them the rules yet.

Did Grackle know the rules? I mean, yes, Grackle knew the rules. But did he really understand them? Was his failure his fault or mine? Who was responsible for Grackle's actions? How much influence did I have? Could I have seen it coming? More importantly: could I have stopped it?

Thinking about Grackle's death, his wings rent from his body, draws my thoughts further back in time, toward Salazar, to the day my mentor and I succumbed to his demands for a death—and a life—that were not legal. I remember trying so hard to get a signal from my mentor, to catch his eyes, to communicate with him. But he wouldn't look at me. I didn't understand it then, but I think I do now. He didn't want any responsibility for whatever I decided to do. Bound and humiliated as he was, I was forced into a position with only bad choices and no right answers. Taking Alejandro Salazar's life when it wasn't mine to take was wrong. But letting my mentor suffer when I was fully capable of setting him free—would that have been right?

I want to believe that the world is full of black and white: ravens and storks. Death and life. But perhaps it isn't that simple. Maybe there's only compromise, gray choices, and dubious outcomes.

If we hadn't taken Alejandro's life, if I had allowed my mentor to suffer and die at the hands of a deranged monster, what would have become of Alejandro Salazar? Would he have woken up from his coma and changed the world? Was he a doctor or a scientist? Was he an engineer or inventor? Would we now have a cure for cancer or flying cars (not that I particularly wish for that, mind you) or some other life-changing, world-altering difference?

Did I remove that possibility from the world all for the sake of one raven?

But if I hadn't killed Alejandro Salazar, would Grackle still be alive? Would he go on a killing spree, taking any life he fancied to assuage a thirst I had no way of knowing he had?

Would the Virago have stopped it? Or would she have let the world run its course?

The interlocking decisions and consequences of my past twirl about me in a dizzying dance, and I can't make sense of any of it. I suppose there's no use thinking about these things; what's done is done. I can't change the past. I can only learn from it.

Though as I make my unconscious way to Carrie's front door, I have to ask myself: what have I actually learned?

I look down at the sleepy tree-lined street that has appeared below me, and my heart skips a beat. I remember this place. I recognize the house next door with its broken garage door and purple curtains. This is the place. Last time I was here, I brought death.

This time, I'm here to deliver news of life. I'm so excited I can hardly stand myself.

And, to my delight, I see her. Sitting on her porch steps with a bowl of candy in her lap, Carrie is wearing a witch's costume, complete with a tall pointy black hat and green makeup. A group of children is tearing their way up her driveway, screaming, "Trick or treat!" as they near, and Carrie stands to greet them, all smiles and compliments on their costumes as she guesses who each is and hands out the candy. She's generous with the chocolate, and the kids ooh and ahh as they look into their bags to assess their loot. And as they run away, Carrie watches after them, smiling.

As I'm settling down, a car pulls into the driveway, the crunch of tires on gravel catching my attention. It's a police car. Carrie makes no move to stand as the car's engine dies and two officers emerge from the vehicle. Carrie's expression is curious, her chin tilted slightly upward, her face bathed in moonlight. The green makeup is unevenly applied. The effect is frightful.

The officers approach, one of them tipping his hat to Carrie as he nears. "Caroline Peterson?" he says.

Carrie sets the bowl of candy aside, frowning as she stands up, arms crossed over her chest. "That's me. Can I help you?"

The officer removes his hat, tucks it under his arm. "Ma'am, is this your home?"

Carrie nods. "It is."

"Is there anyone else inside? Anyone else you might live with?"

Carries shakes her head. "Just my husband, but he's not home."

The officer nods and motions to the door. "Ma'am, would it be all right if we went inside?"

Goosebumps rise on Carrie's arms as she rocks back onto her heels and narrows her eyes. "I'd rather not," she says, her voice grown cold.

The second officer, a woman, steps nearer. "Ma'am, I really think it might be better to do this in private."

Carrie, however, doesn't budge. The first officer clears his throat. "Mrs. Peterson, I'm afraid we have some very bad news. There was a fire out at Soren Home today, and—"

Carrie tosses her head, her body language aggressive. "I heard it on the news," she says. Then, suddenly, her eyes go wide as her mouth drops into a little *o* before she covers it with her hands as she gasps. "Oh, God, you're here about Diana, aren't you? Jesus Christ, is she okay?"

The officers exchange looks, shaking their heads. "Diana?"

"Diana Welland," she says. "She was my roommate at Soren Home. I assume that's why you're here."

The first officer licks his lips and clears his throat again. A nervous habit. "Mrs. Peterson, there was a fire at Soren Home today. Your husband, Jacob Peterson, died on the scene looking for survivors."

A heartbeat passes. Two. Carrie's face loses all its blood, becoming as pale as the moon underneath that streaky green makeup. She begins to tremble, taking a faltering step backward, away from the officers. "Oh, God, no," she says. "Please, no, tell me this is a fucked up prank."

The female officer reaches out for Carrie, who dodges her hand like it's a snake. "We're so sorry, ma'am. He was rushed to Seton Hospital, and the doctors did everything they could, but he was dead on arrival."

Watching a person discover their loved one has passed is like watching a feather fall. The feather descends slowly, nonlinearly, drifting this way and that, suspended by fluid dynamics, yet falling to its inevitable end by gravity. The full dawn of horror often takes a while to arrive, but the end result is always the same. "No. No no no." Her voice is small and onion-skin thin as she shakes her head, squeezing the officer's words out of her mind. "NO!" she screams, stepping forward and slamming her palms into the officer's chest. "He was FINE! He was a good firefighter! He would never have gone into a building if he thought it wasn't safe! Never!"

A heartbeat. Two. And suddenly, like thunder sounding long seconds after a lightning strike, the delayed realization of what has just transpired slams into me, rocking me off my foundation so hard my vision blurs.

I'd followed a firefighter named Jacob into Soren Home.

I watched him search the house, looking for someone.

I'd waited to see if he was a good man.

And then I took his cord into my claw and lifted his soul from his body, ending his life so that I could bring his beautiful soul to Carrie.

Oh.

Oh, no.

Oh, weeping Jesus on the cross. What have I done?

I've killed Carrie's husband.

I remember following Jacob into the inferno, remember him chanting as he dashed up the stairs, coughed his way through the smoke. What was it he'd been chanting? "Die… Die…Die…"

It hadn't meant anything to me, then. They were just sounds coming from his mouth. Something to do to stay focused, to resist the flight urge coursing through the veins. A litany against fear, a psalm of courage.

It had been that, perhaps. But it had also been a woman's name. Not die, die, die, but *Di, Di, Di.*

Diana. Diana Welland. Carrie said she'd been her roommate at Soren Home.

Suddenly, everything makes sense. Carrie had been a patient at Soren Home where she'd roomed with someone named Diana. And, by her expression when she'd spoken of her, she'd cared for this person very much. Perhaps her husband had learned to care for her, too. He'd cared enough to go searching for her, putting his life at risk to rescue her from the inferno.

If he hadn't cared for Diana Welland, would he have rushed into the building? If his wife hadn't suffered from mental illness, would he ever have known Diana Welland? If he hadn't rushed into that building, proving himself a worthy soul, would I have taken his life as an offering for Carrie?

Was Jacob responsible for his own death? Was Carrie responsible? Was Diana? Was I?

I'm so confused by the depth of these questions that when a roaming band of children runs screaming past Carrie's house, I cry out in alarm, losing my balance and jumping from the tree before I fall. I land in the yard in a pile of leaves. The officers and Carrie jump, turn around.

When Carrie's eyes land on me, on the white feathers along my beak, she clutches her chest with both hands and falls to her knees, the animal sounds clawing their way out of her throat rattling against her ribcage. She crumbles into the dirt, heaving and sobbing, lifting her face to me long enough to scream, "Why?"

The officers are sympathetic and sorrowful as they go to lift her up, try to put their hands on her. But she shoves them away, hysterical. "*Why?*" she screams again.

I blink, my expression blank. *Why? Isn't it obvious? Because you asked, Carrie. Because you asked.*

Do you know what you have done?

Is the irony lost on you?

A baby is waiting for you, just like you asked. It's just that now you have no husband to bring it to you.

CHAPTER SIXTEEN

December 4th

IN THE GRAY WEEKS THAT FOLLOWED, I didn't go back to work. I visited cemeteries instead. Longhorn Cemetery, All Saint's Rest Home, Bridgewater State Memorial Park. I plucked wildflowers from highway shoulders and open fields, carting as many manzanitas, tie vines, bitterweeds and buffalograsses as I could to as many graves as I could. It was small solace to me and probably did nothing for the deceased. The people in those graves were on the Far Shore, blissfully unaware of what we endure here.

Even in a legal death, Jacob would have already forgotten Carrie. But now that I'd put him in a boat at the canals for deployment, I really didn't know if she'd ever see him again. Maybe his soul would rot there forever.

That thought made so miserable I sincerely considered suicide. But as I sat in the road waiting for an oncoming 18-wheeler to pulverize me, my baser survival instincts surged center stage, and I flew away at the last second.

Too chickenshit for that, then. The worst kind of hypocrite. Jesus.

I found a piece of glass on the side of the road and took it into my beak, thinking that the magpie might want it, and I could use her company. But when she tried to tell me that she had a message from the Virago, I flew away before I could hear it. She could have flown after me, but she was too captivated by the glass to bother.

The magpie wasn't the only bird who tried to cajole me into going back to work. I ran into other ravens who claimed the Virago had sent them to gently suggest I cross over and stay for a while. But I ran away from those meetings, absconding into the sky and flying faster and farther than they were willing to follow. I avoided jackdaws sitting on flagpoles and blue jays who sang prettily from the trees overhanging the Greenbelt. Anyone who vied for my attention I saw as a potential enemy, or worse, a vessel of reason. I didn't want to hear anything they had to say.

I knew I couldn't run forever. But I would run for as long as I could before guilt pressured me into returning home and facing whatever fate was waiting for me there. I would run until I was exhausted, until I was broken, until I could bear to look at the ground where Grackle had lain covered in blood and gore, where Salazar, too, had met with his final end.

Thinking of Salazar fills me with nostalgia and, for a reason I can't articulate, I find myself wondering how the other Salazar's story ended. The miserable fuck we let live. Perhaps it hasn't ended at all, and he's still living on the east side, conjuring veils, coughing up bloody offal and chatting with dead people, living the unnatural life he sold my soul to obtain.

But I don't feel anger. What I feel is curiosity.

It's December now, and real cold is finally descending over the city. The storm-clotted sky is the color of ash thinned with water. Bracing wind moves through me as I soar eastward, heading vaguely in the direction of the Ordo Templi Orientis. It's been so long since I was last there, and the city has changed so much over ten years. Lots that used to be empty are now retirement homes. Horizons that used to be clear are now choked with high-rise condominiums. Neighborhoods that used to be ramshackle and poor now teem with young, white entrepreneurs zipping around town in electric cars.

It's a nearly hopeless endeavor, and I know it. The east side has changed perhaps most of all as lower-income families have been priced out of their homes to make way for new sushi restaurants, yoga studios, and craft breweries. I don't even recognize the streets in this part of town. Still, I keep flying, hoping for anything that will tug on the back of my brain, triggering my memory and leading me to the place where everything, in retrospect, changed.

I don't so much see it as feel it. A hum in my belly and an electricity in the air that causes my feathers to stand on point. The current feels different, too: pricklier than before, less smooth. I sniff, and the air smells of ozone, though that could be the storm rolling in. I don't think so, though; I recognize this smell.

It smells of magic.

I follow my nose to the end of a street that looks nothing like it did ten years ago. Even the headquarters of the Ordo Templi Orientis has undergone a transition. The building is covered in street art, and in the front yard, immense steel structures that pretend to be an art project erupt from the ground, casting dark shadows along the sidewalk. If not for the reek of magic surrounding this place, I don't think I would have recognized it.

But as I close in, descending lower to make my approach, I see something that I *do* recognize. She's so out of context that it takes me a moment to place her, to recall where I've seen that face. She sees me, too, and a smile curls over her lips, reaching all the way up to her glittering gray eyes that match the color of the sky.

I've seen this woman before. But I can't have seen her

before, because she's dead. Or, more accurately, she was dead when I met her, so I can't be seeing her *now*.

Either way, she's sitting in a rocking chair on the porch of the Ordo Templi Orientis, deep in the thick magic that surrounds her, still wearing her "World's Best Grandma" t-shirt.

It's the woman from the City of Departures. The one who told me how to find the birth canals.

She reaches out a plump hand and beckons me over with a wave. When I'm close enough, she says, "You haven't been home in over a month. Come over here and keep me company. You wouldn't come to me. So I came to you."

I land not so close that she could reach out and touch me if she wanted, but not so far that it looks like I'm keeping my distance. The magic in this house has already made a fool of me once; I have no intention of being tricked again. When the woman sees my hesitation, she throws her head back and laughs, a good belly laugh that rumbles the floorboards. "Oh, don't be like that. Here. I brought you something."

She reaches under the blanket draped over her knees and pulls out a bottle of cider. She pops off the top and holds it out to me as though I can actually take it from her. When I don't move, she cocks an eyebrow and takes a swig. "I believe you said if we ever saw each other again, we'd catch up over drinks. Didn't you say that?"

I hold my tongue. I might've said that. It sounds like a joke I might make. But of course, I didn't mean it. How could I? What chance was there that I'd come across that particular dead woman ever again?

As if sensing my confusion, she laughs again and sets the bottle down. "Honestly, Raven, I thought you'd have figured it out by now. I sent you messages. At least a dozen. Why haven't you come home?"

I stare frankly at her, my beak clicking open as the word drips from my tongue. "...Virago?"

She folds her hands on her ample belly, her shoulders quaking with her suppressed giggles. "Of course it's me. Who did you expect?"

"I didn't *expect* anyone. I came here to see..." I let my words trail off with a little shrug. It seems so ridiculous now.

She grunts, nodding her head toward the front door. "You came to see Salazar. Yes, I know all about that ruse he pulled," she says, seeing my expression. "He's not here. This isn't the OTO anymore; it's grad student housing. The OTO has moved on to bigger and better, just like everyone else. Well, except the poor saps who got gentrified out of their homes. Can't make omelets without breaking a few eggs."

I frown, fluttering my wings in irritation. Plus, it's cold, and the chill has accumulated around my feet, inching up my legs. "Where is he? What became of him?"

The Virago seems to think about this a moment, though I'm sure she already knows the answer. So perhaps she's only thinking of whether or not to tell me. "Does it matter? It was a long time ago. What happened here...You may as well forget it and move on. Dwelling on what's done does no one any good."

I hang my head and let out a low sigh. "I would if I could. But these past few weeks, all I can do is think about the mistakes I've made. Some of them seemed small at the time, or maybe they didn't seem small, but I thought I didn't have any other choice. But looking back, I did have choices. Everything I did was my own choice. Nobody was making me do those things." I lift my eyes to meet hers, compelled to admit the one thing I hoped I would never have to say aloud. But I can't keep the secret anymore. "I haven't come home because I did something despicable, and you're going to hate me for it, maybe even destroy me. I thought I was doing the right thing, but in the end, it didn't matter."

The Virago waits patiently for me to continue, her expression warm and open, which only makes it more difficult for me to get the words out. I take a deep breath and brace myself against the words I have to speak. Here goes everything. "I took a life that wasn't mine to take. A woman asked me to bring her a soul for a baby, and I took her up on it. I found someone willing to risk his life for others, and I thought he'd be the right one. I thought, you know, that he wouldn't be bitter about his death, that he'd be reborn as a wonderful son for this…this damaged woman. But the man I killed for her turned out to be her husband."

The Virago nods, no judgment in her expression. Then, in the gentlest voice, she asks, "And why did you do that, my old friend?"

I shrug. "I don't know. I wanted…She seemed so sad. I wanted to make her happy."

The Virago lowers her chin, but her eyes don't leave mine. "That's part of it," she says, her voice low. "But that's not the *real* reason, is it? Why did you *really* do it?"

The memory of the day at the Renaissance Festival blooms in my mind, and simultaneously I smell turkey legs, hear laughter and applause, and feel a lightness in my chest that I haven't felt before or since. I recall how I'd taken the place of a raven named Arnold who preened and did tricks for snacks and applause. I'd felt so different then—so *wanted*. I'd cherished that feeling, clung to it. I'd done everything to try to relive it, to have someone cheer for me, to whistle and chant my name. Everything including killing a man.

"I wanted to be celebrated," I whisper, shame making me drop my head again. "I've only done one thing my entire existence—bring death and grief and mourning. No one lights up when they see me. No one welcomes me with open arms. No one ever says how happy they are to see me."

"I do," the Virago says.

"Well, you don't count!" I snap, my words tumbling out of my mouth before I can catch them. "You're not like them! You're happy to see everyone! Everyone and everything is all equal to you! Death, life, joy, grief, ugliness, beauty. You love it all! So your opinion hardly matters, does it? You can't possibly know how I feel to be this reviled thing that everyone hates! You can't possibly understand the fantastic worth that *I don't have!*"

She is silent a moment before she says, "You think you have no worth?"

I sniff and turn my head away from her. "I *know* it," I say.

The silence stretches out between us as rain begins to fall. I don't particularly feel like getting wet and so even though I'm angry at her, I step closer to her rocking chair where the roof shields me from the storm. Finally, the Virago speaks.

"I went to great lengths to teach you this lesson," she says at last. "Everything in my universe has value. Everything in my universe is worthy. Everything in my universe is exactly as I planned it to be."

"*Your* universe," I huff, rolling my eyes at the idea. In the distance, thunder rumbles as if agreeing with me. "Did you plan for me to take a man's life without your permission?"

I am absolutely not prepared when she says simply, "Yes."

I am so stunned that I just gawk at her, unable to force myself to make sounds. The Virago, for her part, doesn't giggle at my bug-eyed, slack-jawed countenance; in fact, she looks wilted. Tired.

"Raven, do you *really* think that you did all of this without my knowing? You think I was just too busy to notice that you *smuggled a soul* into the Great Beyond? I orchestrated this entire thing, right down to the first time you met Carrie and took her child away two years ago. Right down to her lack of veil sickness and her ability to see through your death skin." She smacks her lips and reaches for her cider, taking a deep swallow before continuing. "Even Zelda here—this body I've mimicked today. You think you just *happened* to run into a woman who knew exactly how to get to the birth canals? That wasn't chance, old friend. That was fate."

I blink. "The woman was you?"

The Virago laughs and shakes her head. "No, of course not. That was Zelda Fitzpatrick who died in 2005 of hypothermia while camping in the Andes. She really does sneak into the canals to visit the babies. Once I caught her trying to put two into a vessel together; she said they'd make cute twins. No, my point is, I put her there so you would find her and talk to her. That meeting was arranged."

Her words ring like bells in my head, and I can scarcely keep the astonishment out of my voice. "And the fire? The woman Jacob was searching for?"

"Yes. I even made sure to leave the earring at the park so you would visit the magpie who would send you to the Renaissance Festival where you would perform for a big crowd and get that feeling in your bones that you were meant for something larger. But there was reason in it. You needed to know your worth. And only by having you go after what you *can't have* and *can't be* could I get you to see the true beauty in being a reaper."

It's going to take me a minute to process this curling logic. While what she's saying seems ridiculous, I've seen with my own eyes how the Virago peels herself into thousands of pieces, pursuing endless activities, seeming to be in a zillion places at once. But when I really think about the magnitude of what she's saying, I can't wrap my brain around it. The multitudinous threads she would have to weave just to lead me to this place seems…well, like an enormous waste of time.

But then another thought occurs to me. "Wait a minute. If you knew I was going to take Jacob's life…did you also know Grackle was going to follow and see me? Did you know he was going to—"

"If you let yourself think too long about all of this, you're only going to come to hate me," she says, her eyes clouding over as sadness returns to the hills of her cheeks, making them sag. "You'll start to wonder why I let those children die, why I let the other ravens die in cages with their wings ripped off. You'll start to doubt that I'm any good at all."

She's right about that, but I can't let it go. I need to pick at this line of conversation a little bit more. "*Are* you any good at all?"

The Virago crosses her arms over the abundant chest she's borrowed and leans back, causing the chair to rock. The rain is coming down in sheets now, and with the chill in the air, a little cloud has gathered around us, making the Virago look diffuse and dreamlike. Like she's under a veil. "I'm neither good nor bad, Raven. I just am. You want me to be good because we're friends—birds of a feather. I give you assignments, and you carry them out. You don't want to think that I could be anything other than good, because if I'm not good, then what does that make you? But I just am, old friend. As you are just you. Death is both necessary and proper, even when it hurts."

I snort, shaking my head. "I never get to see anything proper in what I do. Just the gloom and misery of those left behind."

The Virago narrows her eyes at me. "Is that so? You've got a selective memory, then. What about that family I sent you at the Governor's Mansion? What did her son say as he stood over her?"

That was the day Grackle took the old woman's soul before the family was done saying their goodbyes. Her death is especially poignant in my memory, and I recall the son standing over his mother, her hand clutched in his.

I nod and take a sharp breath. "The son said he was glad his mother was going on to a better place," I say, still nodding, recognizing the significance of that. "She was old, sick, and suffering. By dying, she wouldn't suffer any longer."

"That, plus she has friends and family on the Other Side. You see how happy the new arrivals are when they meet their entourage. Sure, they're confused at first, but you've seen their faces. And how about all the people you saw in the City of

Departures? Drinking beer, dancing, launching paper bag balloons—did those people look miserable to you?"

I didn't see anyone launching balloons, but I have a feeling that's beside the point. "No," I admit.

"Damn right. And who brought them there? Who was responsible for that?"

I don't need to answer. She's made her point. "But Virago, I wanted to experience the joy of bringing *life*. Is that so wrong?"

The Virago sucks her teeth and rolls her eyes. "You think *that's* always a gas? Ask the thirteen-year-old who gets pregnant by her uncle. Or the family with a sister in a coma while the bills are mounting up. You tell me that those people want to talk about the joy of *life*. Those people are *praying* for death. Come on, Raven. You know how this goes. Cancer cells kill their host by multiplying too quickly. Overpopulation taxes natural resources. All things must exist in a delicate balance: too much life will devour itself. Creation cannot exist without destruction. The sculptor creates art not by adding to the slab but by removing pieces from it. The excavation is as important as what is left behind. This duality is the fundament upon which the entire universe rests. You, my friend, are the sculptor."

A sculptor. Not a garbage collector. The subtraction that leaves room for growth. I hadn't looked at it that way, and suddenly I feel ashamed for my myopia. "But why couldn't you just have *told* me all of this instead of setting up this elaborate scheme?"

The Virago chuckles, her eyes straying now to something in the distance. "Would you have believed me? You needed to see for yourself what happens when you deny who you were meant to be. The question you have to ask yourself is: would the children, or Jacob, or Salazar, or Grackle still have died if you'd just trusted that you were on the right path for yourself from the start?"

"That's a dirty question, Virago."

She nods. "It certainly is. But existing is a dirty business, old friend. Tell me. Did you read the letter of commendation I sent along with Grackle?"

I frown. "The letter...? Oh. No. I never did. I figured it was the same standard bullshit."

The Virago sighs. "You should have read the letter."

We sit together in silence as the rain falls around us, and eventually, the sound of rain and thunder fills in the gap between us until we find the easy intimacy that we used to share before I went and screwed everything up by wanting something I was never intended to have. They say the truest sign of aged love is when people can sit together in comfortable silence without feeling the need to fill it with idle chatter. If that's true, then the Virago and I have conjured a love to last many lifetimes.

The time between the lightning strikes and thunder rolling is shrinking, meaning the storm is getting closer. The Virago clears her throat and beckons for me to come to her. I fly into her lap and nestle into the blankets and allow her to stroke my feathers, which feels very nice even if it does make me feel like a house cat. But this is a special occasion, and if the Virago wants to stroke my feathers, I'll let her.

It's a while before the rain slows down and the thunder and feather-stroking stop and I think the Virago has fallen asleep. But when I turn to look at her, I find I am alone in the rocking chair, and the Virago is gone.

I burrow deeper underneath the blankets until I am shrouded in wool, which is nice and toasty even as the temperature continues to drop. As I'm creating my warm little hovel within the cloth, I feel something cold against my foot. I look down to find a silver ring with a shining amethyst stone. Not a trinket with any real value, but I can't help but smile. I know exactly who this treasure is intended for, and for the first time in weeks, I'm looking forward to paying her a visit.

CHAPTER SEVENTEEN

December 5th

LAST NIGHT'S RAIN HAS WASHED away the pre-holiday jitters that descend over the city every year. I awake with newfound energy and a lightness I've not felt since I danced as Arnold at the fair. Thinking of Arnold and my visit with the Virago, I remember what she said about the letter.

It's buried under the sticks and mud that I've used to create this nest. Long forgotten, it's waterlogged now, and I'm not even sure I'll be able to read it. But I dig until I find it, and when I do, I ease it out by a corner, careful not to rip the soggy mess. I spread it on the branch before me.

In the Virago's swirling, beautiful hand, she's written simply:

"Neither magpie nor raven, man nor woman can receive aught without an equivalent sacrifice somewhere made. There ain't no such thing as a free lunch."

I read the letter several times. I know what she means now,

I think, but I wouldn't have understood it when she sent it. It wouldn't have changed anything.

But maybe that is precisely the point.

The air feels fresh, green, and alive as I take to the sky with renewed vigor. Even traffic on the highways seems lighter. The snaking trail of cars that winds through the hills via the Capitol of Texas Highway usually crawls along as though the drivers have nowhere in particular to go. But today, the cars move along at a quick clip, zipping through the hills like their tailpipes are on fire.

With the silver ring clutched in my claw, I take the long way to the magpie. I don't hurry to her, because I don't know where she's going to send me, and I'm not quite ready to relinquish this delicious calm that I've soaked up since last night. There were moments in our conversation where I wanted to be angry or appalled or disgusted with the Virago, but she was right about one thing: I wouldn't have listened to anything she had to say regarding my feelings of inadequacy. Her methods may seem unnecessarily complex to me, but what do I know? I can barely see over the horizon of my own life. The Virago has a bird's eye view over the entire universe.

I soar down to the south side of town, heading out to Mary Moore Searight Park. This time of year, there aren't as many frisbee golfers about, though I do see a handful of couples holding hands and smooching. There's also a small band of city workers teetering on ladders as they hang Christmas lights from leafless trees, winding them around the bare branches. I make a mental note to come back at night to see them all lit up. I bet it's beautiful.

I find Magpie exactly where I think she'll be, chirping happily in a nest she's just finished building. It's much larger than her last one; it has to be to accommodate the treasures she's amassed. When she sees me, she looks hopeful but reserved. That breaks my heart a little, but it's fair; the past several times she's tried to talk to me, I've been distant or downright rude.

As I approach, I hold the ring out to her so she sees it clearly, and I smile all the way to my eyes so she recognizes it for the peace offering that it is. Now her eyes light up, and she begins to dance, fluttering her wings in vibrant anticipation.

"Raven!" she trills, hopping from foot to foot and nudging me genially with her beak. "Did you bring that for me?"

"Of course I did," I say, dropping it at her feet. "I found it on the east side yesterday; I immediately thought of you when I saw it."

She bends her head low to get a better look; the glittering purple jewel catches fire in her eyes. "Oh, she's a stunner," Magpie coos, clucking her tongue in appreciation. "An absolute beauty. You say you found it on the east side? You didn't get caught in that storm last night, did you?"

"I did, but it was actually quite nice. I had a talk with the Virago."

The magpie's eyes go round as oranges when she hears this, her beak parting slightly as she takes in a little breath. "She was here? You *met* her?"

My brow furrows, and I cock my head to the side, frowning. "Well, it wasn't the first time. Of course I met her. I meet with her every time I take a soul up to the Other Side. Hold on." I squint at the magpie, trying to understand. "You bring me messages from her all the time. Surely you've met her before as well."

"Oh, no," the magpie says, aghast. "I've never met her myself. I get all my messages for you from the crows."

That's definitely news to me. "You—what?! Really? So then how do you know those messages are real? I thought we had better quality control than that!"

The magpie chirps in astonishment, her eyebrow shooting up in surprise. "Are you not feeling well? You know the answer as well as I do. Crows deal in truths."

As soon as she says it, I feel stupid. Magpies deal in treasure, blue jays in promises, jackdaws in secrets, ravens in death, and crows in truths. If a crow tells you that the Virago has a message for you to deliver to your friend Raven, you can bet your bottom dollar that's the case.

"Well, learn something new every day," I say with a shrug. "At any rate, yes, I had a nice chat with the Virago last night. I'm pretty sure she's the one who left that ring for you. I was going to tell you to thank her next time you see her, but sounds like that's a moot point."

"Well, you can thank her for me next time *you* see her," Magpie says. She gazes out over the park, her eyes landing on the workers hanging lights. "It'll be Christmas soon. It's your busy season, isn't it?"

I nod, surprised she remembers. "Yeah. All the suicides."

She pauses a moment as though searching for the right words. Then, delicately, she asks, "Do you think you're ready?"

She looks so beautiful right now, her concern for me making her face glow, and if I could, I would kiss her. But it wouldn't be appropriate, and anyway, beaks are lousy for kissing. Believe me, I've thought about it. I just can't see how it could work. But the idea is indeed lovely. "It's really nice of you to ask, but yes, I'm ready."

"Are you sure?"

I nod. "Pretty sure. We talked about it last night. I mean, the Virago and I. I think we reached an understanding."

Magpie smiles at me, heaving a relieved sigh. "I'm so glad to hear that," she says. "Because...the crow was here last night. He had a message from the Virago."

I whistle. "Already? She didn't waste any time, did she?"

The magpie titters, fluffing her feathers in a fuss. "I guess not, but I'm not one to judge. Anyway, she says you're to head out to Marble Falls. There's a pig farm out there, just on the outskirts. That's all I know," she finishes.

I lean forward and brush my white cheek feathers against the magpie's face. It's the closest thing to a hug I can offer her. "Thank you, Magpie. And I really mean that. Thank you."

"You're welcome. And Raven?"

"Yes?"

She smiles. "Thank you for the ring."

I launch myself into the sky, heading northwest toward Marble Falls, wondering about the circumstances that await me at a pig farm. It could be anything—heart attack, old age, infected wound, tractor incident, home invasion gone wrong. Whatever the case, someone's time on Earth is ending. And while it may be sad, it's also a necessary transition. The newly dead will leave an opening for new life, which, too, will eventually die in an endless cycle of mortality. But that's as it should be. Because if nothing died, nothing new could take its place.

And wouldn't that be sad?

For the first time since I met Carrie, I feel like myself again: whole and complete and necessary and important. I do not feel like the vile little beast I had come to believe I was. I am a bringer of change, of turnover. I am the cleansing of the wound that makes space for healing. I reap what is sown to nourish those left behind. I am beautiful, I am needed, I am loved.

I am a raven.

And I kill people.

www.ingramcontent.com/pod-product-compliance
Lightning Source LLC
Chambersburg PA
CBHW030426120726
47903CB00003B/837